Content Warning

Scream for Me is a dark monster romance and not suitable for all readers.

For a full list of content warnings, please visit gmfairyauthor.com

Scream
FOR ME

A DARK MONSTER
LOVE STORY

G.M. Fairy

Copyright © 2025 by G.M. Fairy

All rights reserved.

The story, all names, characters, and incidents portrayed in this production are fictitious. No identification with actual persons (living or deceased), places, buildings, and products is intended or should be inferred.

Book Cover Art by NSFSANTI

First edition 2025

ISBNs: 979-8-9996915-1-4 (paperback),

979-8-9996915-2-1 (e-book)

If your first monster crush had an oddly similar voice to John Goodman, this one is for you.

CHAPTER 1: DARKNESS

He screams for me—barely a rattle against his brittle ribs. The veins in his eyes burn against the white. His dry lips hang wide. His chest barely moves with a breath. He could have lasted longer. If only I fed him, if only I didn't crush him to a pulp, but hunger takes over all reason. His feeble squeals do nothing for me. I must feed.

Hunger. Hunger. Nothing but hunger exists.

I continue to squeeze. Breaking, crying. It's not enough.

Silence. I roar. Red all around me.

I must find another. Must find more terror. Darkness overtakes me, and my mind blanks. All I see are objects, sources of sound. I know my way to the portal. It's instinct. If only my hunger could be sated in my realm. If only I didn't waste time traveling to the other side. The pain drives me, moving me forward to my reprieve. It hurts to move, hurts to think, but I can't rest. I can't stop until I get more screams, more fear.

It's never enough. I barely remember the day before; the only constant is hunger. Every human barely sates the roar within me, but I must feed. I must fill the ache.

I race through the woods, barreling past limbs pulling my fur, my tail pounding the ground behind me. I must get to the portal—the source of substance. I must find another.

I can only hope that the next soul screams louder and longer, filling the hollow depths inside me. It will never be enough, but I can only feed, only hope for an end to the darkness.

Chapter 2: Marie

Someone else may look at the dilapidated brownstone with "fuck ur mom" spray-painted in bright red letters over the front door and see despair. I am not that person. With a cardboard box in tow and the rest of my few belongings stored in my beat-up car parked behind me, I see a start to my new beginning. I sigh—that stereotypical kind that the main character does at the start of every romance movie—and walk up the cracked front steps and into the building.

Sure, it smells like weed and stale cigarettes, but so have most places I've lived. At least this one is all mine. I climb the metal staircase, barely noticing the muffled shouting from every other door I pass. Even with the obvious signs that this place is not the diamond my heart tells me it is, I still can't believe the incredible deal.

I get to my door, dropping the box and fishing through my pockets until I find the key the landlord gave me the day before. My eyes water a bit once I swing the door open, the stale smell overpowering even for my seasoned nostrils. It doesn't push down my smile, though. I kick my box inside and open the window across the room. Car horns and profanities greet my eardrum like the tweet of storybook songbirds.

No, I'm not on drugs. As I scan the water-stained ceilings and cracked walls, I know this place is shit, but to me, it's home. My home and my home alone for the first time in my life. My childhood—at least the short time I can remember—consisted of foster and group homes. Once I aged out, I lived with random roommates, never finding a pairing that led to a lifelong friendship or anything positive—instead, only broken plates and stolen clothes. When I saw this listing, I initially thought it must be a scam, but I was desperate enough to consider it. I investigated with pepper spray in tow and discovered it was legit.

This one-bedroom, one bath in New York City was mine, all for only 400 dollars a month.

With this amount of savings on my housing, I won't have to take on extra shifts at the diner. I'm used to little sleep, but night classes three days a week, on top of working full-time and finding space in my schedule to study, have been draining the life from me. This place is my haven—a chance for me to get on my feet and crawl out of the despair and poverty life has dealt me.

No more time to gawk and imagine my brand-new beginning, time to finish moving my stuff inside before someone breaks my car windows and robs me. It only takes five trips before I've carried everything up to my room. I barely have any furniture, just a folding table and chairs, a thin rolled-up mattress, and a beanbag. I'm carrying in the last box of kitchen supplies when the door next to mine swings open.

"Oh, hi! I'm Marie, your new next-door neighbor."

The older woman sizes me up and down. "You moving into 805?"

"Yes!" I reply, still smiling.

"Shame."

"Excuse me?"

"You're a pretty young blonde. People who move in don't last long here." Don't know what my hair color has to do with anything, but I guess she's mentioning it as if it's a symbol of my innocence. Oh, if she only knew how wrong she was.

My heartbeat quickens and my body hums. "What do you mean?"

The woman sighs, locking her door and stuffing her keys into her purse hanging from her shoulder. "There have been five tenants in this place in the past ten months."

"Oh, well, you don't have to worry about me. I'll be a good neighbor and always pay my rent on time."

"Been all types coming in and out of here. Sure, most have seemed like addicts, but still, it doesn't add up. I think your place is cursed. The police stopped asking me, but I always tell them the truth. The same thing always happens before they disappear. Loud screaming in the middle of the night and then nothing. Yelling and fighting are usual here, but this is different."

I size her up. I don't know how she wants me to respond, and I'm unsure if she's just a neurotic neighbor. Of course, her story would explain the ridiculously cheap rent. I can't deny the fear zipping through my body, the buzzing that makes me cross my legs just to contain myself, but reason overpowers my squirrel-like instinct. I don't believe in curses or shit like that. Life is hard enough. Almost all bizarre coincidences can be explained by science. The missing tenants of my apartment—if her story is even true—could all be due to addiction, gang violence, or other illegal activity I'm more than happy to avoid.

I sigh, turning my smile back on. "Well, thank you for the cautionary tale, but I think I can hold my own. I'm sorry, but you won't be getting rid of me that easily. I promise you'll love me as a neighbor. I make a mean snickerdoodle cookie. I'd love to bring some over one day. What did you say your name was again?"

She sizes me up again and scoffs. "It doesn't matter. You won't last a week." She turns and walks down the staircase.

"Bitch," I whisper under my breath, hurtling back into my apartment.

Once I shut the door behind me, I lean against the wall, clenching my eyes and willing my thoughts to clear. I don't believe her story, but I can't help that the old woman's words affected the fearful part of my brain. I'm not a scaredy cat; it's much worse.

My hands shake, and I must ball them into fists to stop them from shaking loose and falling into the waistband of my jeans. I could rub myself off and get the need out of my system, but my attraction to fear is something I'm trying to rid myself of, not encourage. Besides, I have too much unpacking to do to waste my time indulging in self-pleasure.

I've been turned on by fear since my teens. I'm an autassassinophiliac, diagnosed by a real therapist and everything. We've never dived deep into where the kink stemmed from, but it's not hard to imagine the cause. There's probably an event or a whole string of horrible tragedies I endured as a young child that rewired my brain. I could try different types of therapy to uncover the suppressed memories in my psyche, but why the fuck would I want to do that? It feels like a blessing that my brain has saved me from that part of my history, even if I'm left with a completely unsavory taste.

I've only been in a handful of committed relationships, and even with them, I'm too afraid to admit my deepest desire. How ironic. You'd think mustering up my courage enough to tell them would turn me on, but sadly, no. All my sexual experiences have left much to be desired. I don't trust men, probably rightfully so, and much to my dismay, I'm tragically heterosexual. With the information about my deepest desires, they could cause some real harm. It's better that I keep my fantasies to myself, the monsters in my movies, and my battery-operated partners.

Even with my compromises on pleasure, the kink is still one I want to kick. Right now, I'm trying to eliminate any reward for my desires, and so far, it's not going well. As I work on unpacking a box of utensils into the wonky kitchen cabinet drawers, the sun setting and shadows dancing across my walls, all I can imagine is a serial killer barging through my door and pressing me up against a wall. Sure, he'd likely slit my throat and wear my skin, but the events leading up to the horror are enough to make my panties completely drenched.

I grunt, abandoning the box and digging into my purse for my pill container. It's only 7 p.m., but I don't work until tomorrow afternoon. There's no reason to rush and unpack everything right now. I swallow a sleeping pill dry, find my silky blue pajama set in a box of my clothes, change, and shuffle my baby-blue slippered feet to my mattress. I groan after discovering I still need to put on my sheets. After fifteen minutes of wrestling with the corners of my lumpy mattress to stretch the worn fabric of my fitted sheet, I lie on my bed, completely exhausted and ready to let my dreams take me away from my perversions.

It's pitch black when my eyelids drag open. I try to fight the intrusion to my slumber, but the shouting and banging won't let me go. My body weighs me down, and the sleeping pill turns my reason thick and sticky. I register that there's some fight happening outside my apartment, and from the sound of it, it's escalating. My groggy brain fills with scenarios of how the scuffle could end. Someone could set off a gun, sending stray bullets through the thin walls of my bedroom. A normal person would jolt upright, dial 911, and seek cover. I, on the other hand, am clearly not normal. My heartbeat quickens, sending a rush of blood to my swelling clit.

What if the men outside burst through my door and kidnap me, using me as a hostage to settle their dispute? It's unlikely, but my fear doesn't need reason. I let my heavy hands seek out the heat underneath my sleep shorts. I couldn't find my underwear, so the silk of my pajamas rubs against my slick flesh. It's terribly arousing, and I play with myself as the screaming heightens outside.

My breath hitches as my strokes through my wetness increase. I've held myself off for too long. I'm so close to coming, and I've barely just started touching myself. I don't close my eyes, instead searching my room for a shadowy figure I can imagine is a creature lurking in the corner. My vision rests on a large object in my closet. I don't remember what I have stored in there, but I swear, piercing eyes stare back at me, glowing in the darkness. Still, the rational part of me assumes it's just my mind playing tricks on me, using the drugginess of the sleeping pills to make my visions even more frightening and erotic.

I cry out, plunging my fingers into myself as I clench. My mind plays even more delicious tricks, and I swear I can hear the figure grunting and the sound of frantic movements. My fear escalates even more, no longer focused on the very real disagreement outside my door, but the imagined beast waiting to pounce and devour me. I keep my eyes open as I massage my bundle of nerves, increasing my tempo, imagining a hulking monster pressing me against the bed, grazing razor-sharp fangs against my skin. White teeth sparkle in the darkness, and heavy breaths escape large nostrils.

I can't hold back, no matter how long I want this mirage to last. I cup my breast, pinching my nipple, as my other hand strums until I'm drowning in a wave of ecstasy, my blood changing into lava. Another horrible trait of my sexual deviancy is that I'm unable to stay quiet. In the past, with roommates, I've had to gag myself to make sure no one hears me. Now, I'm alone, and there's already a screaming match to take the blame if I let my pleasure free. I scream, the sound coming deep from my belly as my orgasm washes over me. My whole body convulses, my cries coming out in a chaotic, choppy rhythm. It's been ages since I let myself devour my cravings, longer since I let my vocal cords slap against each other.

I'm so lost in my ecstasy that I don't even second-guess when the monster steps out of my closet, looming over me. Giant claws wrap around a member protruding between his hairy, tree-trunk legs. He's still shadowed, only illuminated by the faint moonlight from outside my window and his ever-glowing eyes. Something clings to his hands, coming from his body as he strokes himself even faster. I don't flinch, instead continue to rub myself until I've milked every last drop, screaming until my throat is raw. It's not until the monster roars and a large, warm wetness splashes against my thighs that I come back to this plane of reality.

Holy fucking shit. My throat is too sore to even scream, my brain still trying to catch up. My eyes open, really open, and I make out his features. He bends forward—too tall to stand straight in my room, and two curling horns cage both sides of his crown. He continues to stroke his cock—even in the dark I can tell its massive. His white fangs glint from the low light and heat bellows from his huge nostrils. For a moment, I still let myself believe this could all be a dream, until he lets go of himself, small popping sounds following, and grabs me from the waist and throws me over his shoulder. Reality hits me, as if an ocean of cold water had been poured on my head.

I scream. Not of pleasure this time. Of pure terror. I'm not horny, though. Maybe if I didn't just get myself off, but now, as I claw at the coarse hair covering the beast's back, staring down at the equally hairy tail, I yell in pure fear. It can't be a dream. His claws poke my skin as he clenches me, one hand almost wrapping entirely around my waist, his other cupping my ass. I vibrate with his steps as he walks away from my bed. He grunts and then a whirlwind sound comes from below me. In my struggle, I'm able to pull myself up, turning my body around to see where he's taking me. Instead of a closet floor, a black vortex spins below me.

My bitchy neighbor can probably hear me now, smirking to herself that she told me so. I scream as loud as I can until the monster jumps into the blackness and my consciousness blinks out.

Chapter 3: Darkness

She screamed for me. They always do when I first take them. My hunger persists, but the first scream is always the most powerful, allowing me to think reasonably for a moment, so I can contain my catch and gather substenance to make them last longer. She was different. My hunger is there. Always there. But it's a smaller thorn in my side. I've never felt so light, so clear. But still hunger. Always hunger.

The initial pounce always arouses me—that's nothing new. My member stands proudly between my legs, and my attachers move wildly, searching for flesh to hold—to contain. In the past, after my first fill, I've sated my primal urges on my own, but it's always after they scream, when they're unconscious, and I wait for them to wake so I can continue my reign of terror. My hunger always wins. No other feeling. Nothing gets past.

This time was different. This time, I couldn't contain my desire. I had to stroke myself as I watched the female moan, smelling the delicious scent of her arousal. I was starved, but my aching cock overpowered my innate reaction to pounce. And then she screamed, a different kind. It rushed over me like a balm, sating my hunger in a way I can't remember it ever doing before. I must make her scream for me like that again. I must keep her here so she can scream for me forever.

She lies on the stone floor of my cave, the pulsing green lights illuminating her small form, her hair aflame. I made sure not to touch it—the light color I know deep in my bones to stay away from. The light burns. The light is bad. But she doesn't seem bad. Her screams are delicious, and the soft golden hair flowing from her head begs me to grab it and wrap it around my fist as I pound my cock into her, yet I resist. The burn alone wouldn't be worth it.

There's a new hunger growing, one I'm not used to, and something inside of me tells me there's only one way to fill the ache. She can't scream unless she's awake. There's no point entering her if I can't get my fill, although I want to.

I've never thought so clearly after bringing back a human. Usually I throw them to the floor, barely having enough reason to gather a small shell of water from the stream nearby for once they wake. Keeping them alive as long as possible is ideal. Traveling exerts energy, making the hunger stronger.

When I brought her back, I saw my home anew. I laid her down in the corner, positioning the cage of bones around her. I dug through a pile of items left over by the humans. I found two bars that smelled like food. I don't know how I knew that, but I did. I laid them out for her. The body of my previous victim remained at the back of my cave. I disposed of him, dropping him off the cliff nearby. I never enjoy the way they smell when they're gone. I wouldn't enjoy humans at all if they didn't provide our only form of sustenance. I might enjoy her, though. There's something different about her.

As I stare at her gold hair, I find myself inching closer. Her chest rises and falls, letting me know she's alive and will wake soon. I should sneak up on her, let her stew in her terror while she awaits my arrival, but I can't help myself. I reach through the bars. I shouldn't touch it. I shouldn't touch the light. It will burn. It will kill. But I can't help myself. I caress the soft strands. The pain is immediate, piercing through my fur and my thick skin. I roar, cursing myself, but I can't move away. I claw more of her hair, wrapping it around my hand. Yes, it hurts, but it's good. I need more. I pull, forgetting she's trapped in the cage.

She yelps, but I can't stop. I need more of her pain. Her eyes flutter open, the lashes caging the blue, long and thick. Her lips part, and for a moment, I imagine the sound of her soft moans. My cock grows hard as she wakes. Her eyes focus on me, taking me in as she registers her surroundings. She screams. Yes, this is good. It fills me. But no. It's not the same. I release her hair, moving away from her prison.

She curls into herself at the other side of her cage, screaming and clawing against the bones behind her. For every other victim, this would be good—exactly what I want. But I want more. I want the screams she gave me in her realm—the ones that cleared an ancient fog in my mind. I charge the cage, shaking the bars and roaring. She yells louder, her blue eyes bulging from her head. It's still not good enough. Maybe I should pull her out, break her arm, and jam my cock into her mouth until she vomits. Those screams would subside my hunger, but her screams from before leave me with an ounce of reason. It's dwindling, but I know it won't be the same. Even now, with her fear heightened, her screams do not sate me. It's nothing compared to the euphoria I felt in her cave. I need that again.

I push away from the cage, the bones cracking under my grasp. The presence of her confuses me. I need to leave, clear my head. She doesn't blend in with my surroundings. She's a bright object amongst the decay. She's different somehow. Her screams are different. I need them, and I will do whatever it takes to get them from her, even if I must break her.

CHAPTER 4: MARIE

I'm alone. Somehow, this is worse. When will he return, and what does he have planned for me? I take in my surroundings—the bones, the smell of death—all of it adds another layer to my fear, and not in a good way.

If I awoke in my room, I could convince myself that the monster was a figment of my imagination, but here, I know this isn't a dream. The damp chill permeates my skin, and I curse myself for not going to bed in warmer clothes. Of course, no one imagines being taken from their bed and jumping into a portal. Perhaps this scenario has happened in my darkest fantasies, but still, I never thought it would happen.

He woke me, yanking my hair, roaring, and rattling my cage before slinking out of the opening across the dark cave. I barely got a good look at him, but there's no mistaking that he's the monster from my room.

I might be an autassassinophiliac, but that doesn't mean I'll go idly to my death. Once the shock lets loose of my functions, I examine the cave around me—really examine it. There must be a way out of here. I can't give up yet.

My cage is made of bones. I could wish for animal remains, but I'm no idiot. I see the size of a femur in the top corner and know the truth. Will pieces of me be added to this prison if I can't escape? I can't think like that right now.

The only source of light comes from strange plants growing on the walls—algae, almost. They emit a persistent, neon green glow that barely illuminates the rocky space. A pile of what appears to be random items is next to my cage. On the floor, on the other side of the bone bars, are two protein bars and a coconut shell-looking cup of what seems to be water. He's feeding me and giving me water? The gesture terrifies me further. What is he keeping me alive for? I nearly cry when an ache reaches my core.

This isn't the time. Absolutely not. I stuff the disturbing feelings away and focus.

Perhaps I could find a weapon in the pile next to me. I just have to get out of my cage. I shake the bones, listening for a creak or break, but before I can examine my prison further, thunderous steps sound from the entrance. My eyes and mouth grow wide as I take him in. He stalks closer to me, his gaze murderous, and I back up with each step he takes. It's stupid. There's nowhere to go, at least not now. Not before I find a way out.

He's only mere inches away, and I scream. He hums, as if enjoying it. I let the screams die in my throat, pushing away my panic. The dim green light isn't much more than the moon outside my bedroom in terms of illumination, but I can finally take in his features. He's as terrifying as I remembered—impossibly tall, his body covered in a thick fur, patterned with darker patches. He's built, as if every inch of him is composed of muscle or the same substance that makes up the walls of his cavern. Two ivory horns fold in at the side of his head. His fangs jut out from his lower lip, and his eyes glow golden. I've watched a million horror movies, and yet I've never seen a monster like him. He's engineered to break, to cause terror, to destroy. There's no way to look at him and see anything else.

As I've been watching him, he's been watching me. My heart hammers out of my chest, waiting for his next move. Finally, his arm swings in front of him. How did I not notice it before? Between his legs stands a massive cock. At least it looks like a cock, but it's also completely different. It's the color of his darkest patches and must be the size of my forearm. It juts straight out from him, and the tip glistens, leaking a substance that drips down his shaft. He palms himself, lathering his hand in the gleam before stroking his complete length. I'm mesmerized and horrified by the sight. He's without shame as he strokes himself. But of course he is. I'm his prisoner—his prey—and soon I won't exist.

His eyes droop, shading the gold as he continues his strokes. I'm taking in all of him, lips parted and breath heavy, confused, scared, and unfortunately a little turned on, because yes, I'm a sick fuck. I gasp once I notice the base of his cock. Long, skinny appendages reach out, roaming wildly in the air. They almost look like a plant or mushrooms, but it's hard to make out from a distance. One by one, the pieces of him take hold of his hand, burrowing under his fur and attaching to him, but he doesn't slow. If anything, his speed increases as he pulls against the thin pieces of flesh. I can't help it; my mind wanders. *Oh my god.* Are those used to keep what he's fucking in place?

I shudder with fear, which of course turns into a quaking cunt.

I cross my legs and feel my new arousal coating the inside of my silk sleep shorts. He sniffs the air, groaning with a low vibration as he increases the speed of his pumps. Can he smell me? Does he know how turned on I am right now? This is not good. This is everything I feared would happen if I revealed my perverse desires to a human boyfriend, except he's no human. He's a monster—a monster that clearly kills people.

I gulp, clenching my eyes shut. I try to think of peaceful images—sunflowers, meadows, little white bunny rabbits—but the monster roars and stomps closer to me. I open my eyes as he meets my cage, grasping a bone bar with one hand and with the other continues to pleasure himself. He wants me to watch him, probably demands I do. I'm too afraid to close my eyes again. At first, I try to keep my gaze on his eyes, but his stare eats away at me. He wants to consume me, his stare reveals as much.

My fear is too great, making me uncomfortably hot. I trail down his body, his large pectorals pushed against the bars, his defined furry abdomen, and finally his ungodly enormous cock. I can see it more clearly now. It looks as if it's been doused with lube. The thin, slick pieces of skin attached from the base of him to his hand strain as he pulls harder and faster. His balls barely hang, tight against his body.

I moan, the sight oddly erotic. I can't help imagining what it would feel like for him to slip inside of me. Of course, he'd have to force his way in, make entirely new space, break me into something new. He'd attach to me, holding me in place as he fucked me into delirium. It would hurt, maybe kill me. My useless survival skills don't even stir. It's like I want to be slaughtered, be ripped in half. Tears cloud my vision. I hate myself. I hate the prison of my body and mind, and I hate that I have nowhere to look but in the face of my perversion.

I gasp as large globs erupt from his tip. He roars, the sound nearly piercing my eardrums and shaking the bones surrounding me. His seed spurts onto my prison floor, wetting my feet. It's so much, enough to drown someone if you forced their face into it. I hate that my brain imagines dying that way. I can't look away, even as the need inside me rises in temperature and wetness covers my shorts. I whimper, the torment too much.

I notice something new—growing in size with each spurt from his cock. Another bulge rests above his testicles, not as nearly as pronounced but firm and expanding. I don't need an explanation. I've read enough werewolf smut to know what that is. It's a knot. He has a fucking knot. It all makes sense, the tentacles, the performance before me—he's built for breeding. The question is, does he mate with his kind, or am I a prisoner he can fill with his offspring until they burst through my uterus? I'm not the first human he's captured. It's clear from the remains. If my theory is correct, mothers don't last long in this place.

The tentacle-like attachments, release his hand as if sated. They rest at the side of his cock, hidden by his fur. He lets go of himself, barely shrinking. His member almost nuzzles into his fur, making only the enlarged knot visible. No wonder I didn't notice it when I first woke up. Not that I had much time to examine him.

I return to his eyes, remembering that I should not be so fascinated by the workings of his sexual organs, regardless of what my traitor body craves. His eyes track every inch of me, and his large nostrils flare with angry breaths. Even with my newfound theory, why did he just jerk off in front of me? What's the point of drawing this out? He could have taken me, driving himself inside of me until I ripped, choking on my screams. I try not to imagine it, try to stop the moan clawing at the back of my throat in anticipation. It doesn't make sense, and the uncertainty of what will happen next is a slow and cruel torment. He pushes himself away from my bars, stumbling across the cave and slipping out the opening again. Maybe his plans require the torture, the fear slowly cooking my organs until they're tender and boiling out through my pores.

The air lightens now that he's gone, and the insistent need between my legs lessens. I exhale, so goddamn thankful he didn't make me reveal how much I want the brutality. If he knew, he'd ruin me, and I'd allow it. I at least want to die with some dignity.

I don't know when he'll return, but I need to get the fuck out of here before he comes back. If I don't, I'll likely come just from the sight of his razor-sharp fangs before they rip out my throat.

CHAPTER 5: MARIE

S omehow, I fell asleep. I could kill myself if the monster doesn't get to me first. I spent what felt like an eternity chipping away with a loose stone at a section of brown bone. My eyelids heavied, and my adrenaline wore off.

I jolt upright, the sound of dripping bringing me back to consciousness. Thankfully, I'm still alone, and maybe there's time for me to get out of here. As I take in my surroundings, assessing the corners for any sleeping monsters, I notice a crack in the bone down low. I kick at it, using what little force I have, and to my surprise, it breaks, bending outwards. I keep kicking until I've shattered the bars above and below, and there's enough space for me to pull myself out. A jagged edge scrapes against my stomach, but I don't stop, not letting the pain get to me, even after looking down and seeing the shallow but bloody cut.

I'm free of my cage, but there's no time for relief. I rush toward the pile next to me, immediately finding a worn brown coat and pulling it over my shoulders. I grab two mismatched shoes—one a greyed sneaker and the other a work boot. Both are left feet, and all my items are at least three times too big, but I'm not wasting time looking for something that fits me properly. This isn't a fucking fashion show. Instead, I search for any weapons. Sadly, the items seem like mostly clothing, wrappers, glasses, and various accessories. My heart keeps an imaginary timer, blaring that I've already wasted too much time. I scramble to gather the protein bars near my cage floor and shove them in my pocket. I gulp down the water. It's mineral tasting, and for a moment, I panic that it will make me sick, but I don't have any other choice. Humans don't last long without water, and I don't know how long it will be before I can find another source.

The wind howls at the mouth of the cave. I should be more frightened by what lies beyond the stone prison, but I'm left with no choice but to flee. A part of me hoped that I was still in my world, just hidden in a bizarre pocket of time. I'm in dark woods, but it's obvious I'm nowhere on Earth. Roars and screams bellow in the distance, mixed with high-pitched yells and deep-throated laughs—the sounds of nightmares. It's lighter than inside the cave, but not by much. The same neon-growing algae inside the cave are the only source of light, growing on impossibly tall trees and sparse rock formations. The trees are skinny, offering barely any foliage besides random thin arms protruding out at their bases. I follow the height of the trees, and a black and starless sky stares back at me. It could just be night, maybe light will come soon, but the realistic part of me tells me that's not the case.

The monster is nowhere in sight, but there's no relief. A twig snaps, and something hoots. Up above, creatures swing from tree to tree. Golden eyes stare down at me, each figure owning numerous pairs. I don't waste time getting a good look at the things; there could be five or a hundred of them. I sprint in the direction opposite the cave. A pain disarms me once I pick up speed, and I cover the source, finding my hand covered with blood. I completely forgot about my cut until now, but I can't let it slow me down. I keep running, the figures in the tree howling after me and growing closer.

I have no idea where I'm going. Now my mission is shelter, but I don't see anywhere to hide. A noise grabs my attention to my right. I turn my head but don't stop. It sounds like something is close, but there's nothing there, at least not that I can make out in the low light. It hasn't even been five minutes since I left my prison, and I'm already being hunted. How do I think I will survive much longer? There's nothing else to do but run faster. I can't let myself get freaked out. I turn my attention ahead, praying solace will appear.

The sound next to me grows closer, the ground rustling and labored breaths catching up. Thankfully, the weird multi-eyed monkey things swinging from up above seem to have left me alone. A thunderous roar behind me shakes the ground, followed by a gallop. Multiple beasts are running after me, and one of them has clearly scared away my initial monkey hunters.

Something flings against me, taking me to the ground. I scramble, flipping myself to my back to see my attacker, but nothing is there, even as I feel a scaly weight pressing down on my chest. Blinding colors flash before my eyes, and a new monster materializes. I scream, and the lizard-like creature smiles down at me with razor-sharp teeth. He vibrates a forked tongue, tasting the air, and his large googly eyes wobble in their sockets.

I fight against the beast, attempting to get away, but if his slimy scales and size weren't enough to overpower me, he completely disappears every few seconds. He changes from red to blue to the forest around me. His grip tightens, six clawed hands wrapping around my arms and legs. A seventh member pokes against the center of my abdomen, and I make a quick guess at what that could be.

It's all happening so fast. Thank God because I don't even have time to turn my fear into my dreaded perversion. Perhaps I'll die with my dignity intact after all. I close my eyes, accepting my defeat, but a thunderous roar comes from above me, and I hate to admit I recognize the sound. My insides heat. The weight lifts off me, claws grazing against my skin. Sure enough, my monster—no, my most hated monster—stands above me, the scaly creature flashing colors in his grasp.

"Mine!" he screams as he rips the lizard beast in half, his muscles tensing, gore spilling to the ground. It's the first time I've heard his voice, and it's just as I would have expected, low and terrifying. He drops the severed carcass before focusing his golden gaze on me. His feline snout expands in angry breaths, and it's not until he pounces on me that I curse myself for not making my escape when I had a chance, even if it would have only given me a few seconds' head-start. Instead, I just watched as he tore my attacker into two. "Mine," he almost whispers the word, growling as he sniffs from my ear down my neck.

I push at him. "I'm not yours! Get off of me." It's the first time I've spoken to him, and the words feel foreign coming out of my mouth. There's not an ounce of thanks in me for him saving me from the scaley beast. He just wants me for himself.

He pulls up, holding his top half over me, staring at me with disgust. The small stillness of the moment allows my brain to wander. I notice his weight against me, specifically the pressure between his legs. Something squirms against my leg, and I scream in horror, trying to roll away. It's his weird penis-suction-worms. He doesn't budge; if anything, he presses himself harder against me.

I'm terrified, a feeling I'm growing used to, but unlike the monster before him, my darkness spreads from the corners of my brain until it's my primary focus. Before I can even register, my breath labors, heavy in my chest, as I try to combat the boiling inside. I still attempt to squirm away from him, but my body betrays me, pressing the source of my heat against his.

He sniffs the air, the same way he did in his cave when I nearly dripped down my leg. Of course I'm fucking wet. I groan, rolling my head to the side, furious with myself. He folds himself completely over me again, and his nostrils dance across my skin as if searching for the source. I push at him, but he doesn't even notice; instead, he continues trailing down my body. I hiss once his face grazes against my wound on my stomach. He stops and makes a dissatisfied growl.

I'm an idiot. He wasn't smelling my arousal. He smelled my blood. He's a monster keeping me in a cage of human bones. My sick desires have turned my brain to mush. He doesn't want to fuck and impregnate me; he wants to eat me. Fear drips like an IV into my veins, and I push his shoulders, using all my might to get away. But that's not true, because my lower half arches, pressing myself into him.

The monster sniffs and hums, continuing to trail down my body. When he gets to my shorts, a measly shred of fabric, he rips them off. I cry out, the pain quick and adding to my arousal. He moans, his body shuddering, and I must close my eyes. It's all too much. I don't even register that I'm bare to the elements until I feel his nostrils against my seam. He moans again. "Mine." The words are low and deep. "Can I taste?"

The question stuns me. Did he just ask to eat my pussy? No, there's no way. I must be imagining things. I decide if this isn't real, if I'm just imagining a scenario where I have a say in this, I might as well agree to the thing I actually want. "Yes," I whisper, doubting he can hear me, doubting that it matters. To my surprise, he moves his tongue through my heat as if my hushed word was the spell that broke his stupor. I wasn't crazy. He was sniffing out my arousal, but there's no way he's doing this only because I uttered my approval. I can't believe he wouldn't have done as he pleased regardless of what I said. But as he licks me, his tongue covering every inch of my cunt, from top to bottom, I'm thankful I murmured the word, if anything, to diminish the slight chance that this wouldn't happen, because God, it's good.

He's not gentle, not teasing; he licks rapidly as if my wetness is the sweetest taste in the world. I wanted this. I agreed to this, but I'm still a captive attempting to escape. I don't want to show him how much I'm enjoying his rough tongue slipping through me. I remain rigid, not letting my body melt into him. A small scream spills from my lips, and I clench them as an attempt to stop the sound, but it's too late. He bristles at my noise, licking me more rapidly and holding me tighter with one hand and pressing his weight down on me as his other hand reaches for himself between his legs. The sound of his pre-lubed cock, slipping through his massive hand, takes away the little semblance of my armor. I fall back, relaxing my legs so he can have better access to me.

What's the point in fighting this? I give in to the fear, give in to his massive tongue, stroking from ass to clit. Perhaps this is how I die. He might actually eat me after this, him or something else entirely. What a way to go, though—splayed out on an alien forest floor, bloodied and bruised, with my captor licking me to orgasm, fear coursing to my brain. I've fought my desires for so long. Maybe it's time to give in. A smile forms at the corner of my lips as my nerves lighten and my blood turns to thick honey. Yes, it's so good. What a fucking way to go indeed.

I reach for him, holding onto his horns as a scream comes from deep in my belly. I can hear the speed of his strokes increasing, and moans vibrate against my clit. "Mine," he says, his words muffled against me. I let my vocal cords wail into each other as I ride my captor's face. His tongue never wavers, never loses pressure, and I float to a different realm—not Earth, not this hellscape, but a form of heaven—without judgement of my true nature. For a moment in time, I'm just myself—my fantasies come to life.

He roars against my cunt, and a warm liquid floods under my ass. He came, and the feel of his wetness reaches me; the sheer amount he must have released sends me over the edge. Gone are my memories; gone is anything outside my body. I scream, louder than I have my entire life, letting the orgasm have its way with me.

Before I even float back to Earth—or wherever the hell I am now—I'm pulled off the ground and thrown over a fuzzy shoulder. There's no time to return to my body. Perhaps I died and forgot the torture of being ripped apart, because there's no pain. I blink hard and return to reality. The monster carries me on his shoulder through the forest, running with me. We're not alone, followed by an army of monsters. Each one is different and more grotesque than the next. Some swing from trees, some slither on their bellies, some fly close to the ground, but there's one similarity amongst all of them—all their eyes focus on me as they lick their razor-sharp fangs.

Chapter 6: Darkness

I've never thought so clearly. I've never been so strong, so alive. And it's all because of her. She screamed for me, loud and glorious, returning a part of myself I didn't know I had lost. I just wish I'd had some of my new reason before I licked the sweetness between her legs, and she screamed, vibrating the ground beneath her. Now every wretched soul nearby chases after me, my prize vulnerable over my shoulder.

A howler swings in front of me, brave for its small size. I grab its head, squeezing its many eyes to a pulp in the palm of my hand. He doesn't even get a chance to scream.

She gives a small cry of terror, and I wrap my hand around her middle to steady her. "Don't scream," I order, and surprisingly, she follows my order.

The noises from the beings behind us decrease, and I look back to see them fading into the distance. I've never been so fast, and luckily for me, most of the creatures are smaller and unable to keep up with me. Larger beasts like myself stay confined to their dwellings, jumping through their portals to find their prey. The crowd behind me lives off our scraps. I'm not sure how I know this, and it troubles me that I've unlocked a part of my memory. What else rests inside my murky mind?

She cries out and bangs against my back. I turn to see a crawler gaining on us. This beast is similar to me in the fact that it's large, powerful, and travels through the portal on its own. It must be desperate to try to steal my prey instead of finding its own. Again, I'm puzzled why I know so much about him.

I pick up my pace, darting around trees as an attempt to lose him, but he uses his web, shooting from one of his many legs, to pull himself across the distance between us.

When he's nearly steps away, I know it's no use trying to run. I must fight him off.

I fling my human atop a patch of glowing brush behind me and roar at the crawler. He swipes one of his eight pointed legs at me, nearly slicing me, but I dodge his blow just in time. He hisses, revealing rows of sharp teeth. I barrel forward, using my weight to push his round form off balance and slash across his many eyes. Normally, I don't think I'd be able to topple him and cause him to scream in agony so easily. His legs keep him steady, and the hard, grey shell makes him difficult to injure. But with the newfound power and clarity from her scream, I'm able to attack more effectively, not just based on instinct.

My confidence wavers as pain radiates across my back. I try to use my tail to block him, but I'm too late; he slices through my fur and flesh. The pain distracts me, and the crawler uses it as his chance to push me off him and pin me to the ground. He looms over me, with bloodied eyes and a hooked claw pointed at my throat. I should be dead already, but he speaks, "Give her to me." I can't remember having spoken to someone from my realm, but that's not true. There's a distant memory at the back of the dark tunnel of my mind.

His words ignite a rage within me, sating my pain, and I jump atop him. "Mine!" I roar as I claw at his eyes once more, causing him to wail. He doesn't give up, though. Even while using my legs, arms, and tail, I can't keep his legs pinned to the ground. He rips at my back, causing one avalanche of pain after another. I don't stop ripping into him until I can't take it anymore. I roll off him, and to my luck, he runs off in the other direction, yelping and limping. I could go after him, finish him off, but I'm too weak, my vision blurs, blood drips down my back, and I must keep my human safe.

She's huddled in the place I left her, her head between her knees, still draped in the oversized brown fabric, which makes her almost blend into the environment. I pick her up and yelp, pain taking over all my focus. She gives a small scream. "Shh!" I order. "More will come." She quiets, allowing me to cradle her small body in my arms.

I search for a place to hide, to regain my strength. There's a dark hole at the base of a large stone nearby. I drag myself toward it, placing my human on the ground as I peek into the darkness to see if it's empty. It's a poor decision. My vision gives out, and my consciousness swirls. I'm aware as my body falls after me and my human screams, "No!" from up above.

Chapter 7: Darkness

A soft sound wakes me, a noise seeping from dreams and bleeding into the painful consciousness around me. I swear I've heard it before, a distant memory I can't seem to grasp. The humming pulls me out of my darkness increasingly until I can't ignore the growing ache. I cry out, pulling away from the source, trying to roll onto my back.

"Stop, you'll hurt yourself!"

Her voice holds me in place, and I remain on my stomach, searching my surroundings without moving. We're in a small cave, barely enough room for me to stretch out completely. There's dull light glowing from brush yanked from the ground and positioned around the perimeter, tucked into nooks in the stone wall. She touches my back again, and I hiss, sitting up and grabbing her hand. I pull her over me, and our eyes meet. "I'm trying to cover your wounds," she says angrily, pulling up the shredded small fabric that was previously around her body. Is she bare? I look down, taking her in, but she's buttoned the worn, large brown coat all the way down, hiding her perfect form.

I sit up more, pulling her so she's seated on my lap and wincing as the pain intensifies, the edges of my scratches stretching. "I will heal on my own," I say, resting my head against the wall behind me and closing my eyes, never letting her out of my grasp.

"How do you know?" she asks without even a moment of silence. I open my eyes, studying her furrowed brow, the scrunch of her lips. I've never had a prisoner speak to me in such a manner, at least not that I can remember. Although I never remember any of my past victims, even now, as my true consciousness returns.

I might not know much, but I do know this. "My body always heals on its own. I just need some more time."

She yanks away from my grasp. I don't have the energy to fight her, but even free from my hold, she doesn't move, her legs still straddling my upper thighs, my hidden cock so close to her cunt. Sadly, I'm too weak to grow hard. She crosses her arms. "Why can you talk now?"

Her question puzzles me, and I lean forward out of my slump to ponder it. "I don't know. I think it's your scream. Every time you scream, I regain a part of myself. I gain clarity."

"Why?" She inches closer, her hands on my thigh as she studies me.

My pain vanishes. "I feast on human screams. That's why I capture them. Your screams are different, though." I'm not too weak after all. My cock hardens as her bare cunt grazes against my opening. She shudders, pulling back, but I grab her wrists as I grow, letting my member pierce between her lips. Her eyelashes flutter as her lids melt together, but as my attachers stir and seek out her heat, her eyes pop open and she stiffens. "Stop."

I've heard the word a million times through screams, through tears, through cries. It has never meant anything to me, but now it's different. I don't want to follow her command, but it causes me to pause, and my members halt their search. I won't take from her what's not freely given. A hollow ache in my chest refuses my instincts to claim her.

She shakes away a glossiness in her eyes. "I need to know more. What's your name?"

"Name?"

She sighs. "My name is Marie. That's what people call me. What do people call you?"

Marie. The word covers me like a warm embrace. I want to roll it on my tongue, but she watches me, waiting for an answer. I shake my head. "No one calls me anything." It's the truth, but somehow it feels like a lie, like there used to be a word assigned to me, but I can't remember it.

"Okay, well, where am I?"

The question puzzles me. "You're here."

"Where is here?"

"A hole."

She groans, pushing herself away from me. I growl, low in my throat, but it doesn't stop her. "You took me from my home and brought me to yours. Where is your home located?"

I shrug. "I find my prey through the portal and bring them back to my realm."

"What is your realm? Is it only filled with creatures like you and those beasts that chased us?"

"Yes. There are no humans here. We bring them back through portals so we can feast on their screams. It's how we survive."

She shakes her head as if everything I say is ridiculous. It aggravates me and makes my cock hard at the same time—a confusing mix.

She's still on my lap but straightens, crossing her arms. "Okay. Well, I need you to take me back."

"No."

"Haven't you gotten your fill of my screams? What happens to the rest of your *prey* that you've captured?"

I don't answer, and I can tell she comes to the conclusion on her own. She arches away from me, her eyes grow wide, and the intoxicating smell she always radiates intensifies. I sniff the air, my filaments moving wildly and my mind losing focus. Surprisingly, I gather words instead of driving inside of her. "You can't go back home."

She nods with a large gulp. "Are you going to kill me?"

"No."

"Why not?"

"Because your screams. They're different."

"What if I don't scream for you anymore? You don't scare me." She's lying, but I ignore it.

I shake my head, smirking. "Not screams of fear. The screams you make when you're clenching around air and wishing it were my cock."

She gasps, her eyes wide. "I will *never* scream like that for you again."

I reach forward, pushing my hand between her legs, the moisture seeping between my fur. "Are you sure about that?"

Her breath loses its pattern, and she rubs against me; she doesn't move toward me, so I pick myself up, moving toward her. It's a bad idea; the blood rushing to my cock can't mask my pain. I pull back, groaning.

She leans forward, grabbing my shoulder. "Let me see." Her words hold concern. She's switched from anger to arousal to worry in a matter of mere moments. It makes my head spin. I may have my authentic self back, but it's not enough to understand her.

I close my eyes as she climbs off me and examines my back. "It doesn't look like it's healing. You need to take it easy."

"Why do you care?" I say through the pain. I can't help that her concern lifts a heavy stone in my gut, but I've never had anyone care about my well-being before. Perhaps that's not true—a shiny memory glints in the back of my mind. She obviously wants me inside of her, filling her with my seed, but I don't need to be without pain to do that. She seems troubled by my discomfort and it rattles me.

"There are monsters everywhere in this place. If I have any chance of surviving, I at least need to be around the one who hasn't killed me yet."

"I promise. I won't let anyone hurt you." She's my prize, and with every passing second in her presence, a tenderness grows.

She scoffs. "Yeah, so only you get to hurt me."

I turn to her. "I will keep you safe, but you must stay here with me. I can't take you back. If there were a way I could, I would."

She's frozen, watching me with water-colored eyes. Finally, she speaks. "Why not?"

"It's impossible. You can't go back through the portal, or you'll die." It's a lie. I don't know why I come up with the string of words. I've never tried to take a human back to their realm. I use them until they're void of breath, but I need her to stay. I need her to scream for me. For the first time in my life, I'm not starved. Maybe I could force the screams out of her, run my tongue through her seam, even if she resists. It would work, but for how long? If she accepts me as her only form of refuge—grows comfortable with the idea—she'll scream without me having to use her up until I'm left with nothing but an empty shell.

Tears cloud the sparkle in her eyes. Humans have cried in front of me more than they have not. Usually, it does not affect me, but this time is different. The sight pains me, almost more than the wounds on my back, but not as much, because the pain increases and my vision tunnels—my body demands to rest so I can heal. I settle to the ground as she turns away from me, whimpering. The world grows dark again, and I watch as my one real source of light fades out, her chest heaving with her cries.

CHAPTER 8: MARIE

I watch him sleep, his large chest rising and falling in even patterns. It's the only thing I can do because my whirling mind won't allow me a moment of slumber. I eat half of the protein bar in my pocket, thankful that I managed to keep them after the attack—and the pussy eating. My PJs are gone. My shorts were ripped from my body, and I tore up my cami to stop the monster's bleeding, but I've still got a dead guy's coat—gotta take the little wins. Thank God I downed the water before I left the cave. I'm okay for now, but I'll need more soon.

So much has changed in such a short amount of time. It seems like only yesterday that I moved into my shitty little apartment, but at the same time, it feels like a lifetime ago. I went from hating the monster who captured me to tending to his wounds in a matter of hours. Not to mention screaming as he licked my cunt and then almost riding his dick on my own accord. This must be Stockholm syndrome, and at this point, I welcome it. If what he says is true and that he can't return me to my world, what's the point in fighting him and my urges? He might be my only form of safety.

I can't completely give up hope yet, though. There must be a way back home, or at least somewhere else that is better than where we are. I can't live in darkness, surrounded by terrifying monsters. Sure, my life wasn't fantastic back home, but at least it was mine. For the first time in my life, I had my own home and was carving my destiny. Now I'm a prisoner in a literal hellhole, fighting my disgusting urges to fuck the monster who brought me here. Maybe he's regaining consciousness because of my screams, or maybe he's full of shit. His home was littered with human remains after all. I'm not going to believe *I'm special*, or *I'm the one to change him* so easily. I've seen enough love bombing from narcissistic pieces of shit to have that pulled over on me. One thing is for sure: I don't trust him as far as I can throw him, which says a lot since he's fucking massive. Perhaps he can keep me safe, but he won't needle his way into my bleeding heart, Stockholm be damned.

The monster without a name stirs, softly at first, but then thrashes. He sits up, his golden eyes wild and his hands pounding the walls next to him. "My Marie. My Marie!" he screams, his eyes not focusing on me. I crawl on top of him, making soothing noises. "I'm right here. Calm down."

He registers me, and his giant hands clasp around my waist, pulling me close. He sniffs my neck, a low hum at the back of his throat. "My Marie. My Marie." He whispers now like a prayer. I feel his heart rate slowly return to an even tempo against my chest, but then it speeds up again as something nudges against my thigh. Jesus Christ, this guy always wants to bone. So do I, but he can't know that. I won't let him win, even if I must keep him alive for my survival.

I push him back. "Wait, let me check your wounds."

He growls and snaps me back against his chest, licking at the tender flesh of my neck. "Marie," he says with a hum. It's odd—I can tell he's lost some of his reasoning—lost some of the strange clarity that illuminated his eyes before he fell asleep. He's more of a monster now, unable to form sentences or stop his desires.

He pushes me to the ground and looms over me, his tail pounding against the ground, making tiny rocks fall from above. He sniffs down my neck and shoves his snout down the front of my coat until he nestles between my breasts. "Smell so good."

Great. He smells my fucking arousal again. Now I'm not even able to mask it with the thin barrier of my sleep shorts since he ripped those off and left them in the woods. I'm completely bare under the oversized coat, and as he pulls at the top buttons, trying to gain access to me, I panic. If he rips the buttons off, I'll be buck naked with nothing else to wear. "Wait, let me do it." I squeeze my arms in between us, undoing the clasps before he snaps them off. When my breasts pop free, he gives a contented sigh, sniffing them before lapping at my already pebbled nipple.

I may have given him access, and sure the nipple licking feels nice, but it doesn't mean I want him to fuck me right now. Well, that's not entirely true, but I still try to push him away. "You're going to hurt yourself."

He growls, biting my nipple. I scream, immediately thankful he didn't bite it off with his fangs. At least he's conscious enough to control his pressure. Unfortunately, the sharp pain against my sensitive skin is so fucking good, and my legs slip against each other from underneath him. "Okay, big guy. Maybe we should do this later." My mouth's a fucking traitor to my body, but she's one determined bitch. I don't know what I'm trying to prove and to whom, because obviously, I'm not fooling anyone here.

"Mine." It's barely a word as his giant, slick cock pokes against my cunt. I've seen the thing, still huge in his monstrous hand. Sure, I've dreamed about him stretching me around him, but I don't think it's physically possible. In fact, I'm sure he'll rip me in two.

"Let me in?" His tone poses the words as a question, but I don't believe he'd stop if I asked. I test my theory. "No," I whisper.

He pulls back slightly, glaring and grimacing as if in pain. Will he punish me for my refusal? It terrifies me, and of course, that fear mixes into a strange concoction of desire. I'm weak. Whether I'm truly afraid of the repercussions or I'm too fucking horny. I give in before he can even roll off me or take me anyway—whatever was about to happen next. "Okay, fine. Fuck me." Maybe my terror-induced arousal is a defense mechanism because as my heart quickens and panic rises in my throat, my cunt melts even more, providing more liquid and elasticity for him to make his way inside of me. I doubt my body's wet gifts will do much, though. He's about to obliterate me.

I catch his stare, shining in the darkness of the cave. He studies me now, and I don't know how, but I can tell a part of him has returned. That could be because he hasn't forced his way inside me yet, proving he's not completely deranged, but it's something else, a humanity settling over his fierce features.

I almost welcome him, spread my legs, beg him to do as he desires, but then I feel them—suctioning my legs and crawling upwards. I scream, attempting to kick him away, but his legs hold me down. He leans over, whispering into my ear. "Let me make you scream."

I know what he means. He doesn't want me to scream in fear, but desire. I told him I'd never do that again, but as his stretchy filaments nestle into place—some of them attach to my legs, some to my stomach, one covers my asshole, and another takes hold of my clit—I do as he asks. I cry out, the suction pulsing against me in a gentle but even rhythm. "Holy fuck!" His tentacles hold me in place, some suctioning so hard that I'm sure they'll leave marks, but the ones on my sensitive areas—it's like they're purposely wringing the pleasure out of me. Perhaps they're more helpful in keeping me in place besides only restraining me. I wouldn't move away from this monster even if he took a chunk out of my arm—it's too fucking good.

"Yes, my human. Just like that. Scream for me." He pushes himself inside, a small fraction of an inch. His cock is soaking wet from his own natural lubrication, but

I still burn from the force. The pain doesn't settle over me, though—the pleasure from his filaments massaging me overwhelms my senses, allowing me to stretch. Two of the little guys move off my leg and position themselves on either side of my entrance. They pull back as if making more room. Wow, these things are useful. Creepy, but useful. He pushes in further, this time more easily.

"Oh fuck, yes!" I cry. My legs are wide, wrapped around his waist. I cling to his back, my nails digging into his coarse fur.

He looks down at me, his eyes less golden and more of a burning red. "You like this, little human? You like screaming around me." He pounds in deeper, and the tentacle on my clit quickens.

His words send me over my edge, and I'm a sputtering mess. "Yes!" I scream. I've never come so suddenly, so forceful, and yet it doesn't seem to be over for me, as if a barricade holding back a lifetime's worth of orgasms is just about to tumble.

He leans down, bringing his ear to my lips and cupping my mouth as I scream around his dick, now pushing deeper and deeper. "Good human, taking me so willingly. Do you want more?"

He pauses his thrusts right before he pounds to my deepest point. I'm desperate now. The pressure from his filaments hasn't lessened, making my pleasure never-ending—a continuous wash of ecstasy. I need more, though. I need all of him. I don't know how I've fit him so far, but pain isn't even a concept in my mind. Only pleasure.

"More, please. More." I cry, tears running down my cheeks.

He thrusts into me, hitting as far as my body will allow. It's so sudden that I'm not prepared. I don't expect the pain, don't expect him to reach so far within me. My vision blurs. I'm losing consciousness, but my moans and yells don't stop flowing from my lips. I'm screaming at the top of my lungs now, and I barely register as he wraps his paw over my mouth—almost my whole face. He wants my screams, but he's muffling them.

"Too dangerous. Too loud and too sweet. Your screams are only for me."

I don't know if he realizes it, but he's cutting off my airflow, not enough to kill me, but with my consciousness already tunneling, I'm fading out. He roars in my ear, erupting inside of me and spilling out from the lack of space. I almost forgot about his knot until the pressure of it builds at my entrance. His suctions don't let go of me, even as another explosion goes off in my body. I can't take it. I'm sure I'll die, and as everything washes away, I'm comforted that my death was one I'd only dreamed about in my fantasies—coming into oblivion. Literally.

CHAPTER 9: DARKNESS

My monster-self returns, bright, blinding light taking hold. The need to claim, the need to breed are my only motivations. I don't stop. Even when she quiets, even when her body slackens, tiny slaps against the floor as I slip in and out of her, not until I've released every last drop of my seed and my knot expands fully. I hold myself over her, catching my breath, waiting to deflate, and doing my best to still the spinning walls around me. Finally, everything settles—really settles. I don't remember feeling so clear, so myself. With the clarity comes self-loathing. I take in the small form underneath me, my insides squeezing around my bones.

I caress her face. My Marie. At first, I think I've killed her, lost myself and fucked the life out of her. But as I catch the rise and fall of her chest, I sigh in pure relief. She's just unconscious. Not that this sight thrills me either, but it's better than dead. Anything is better than dead. I examine her to see if I've damaged my precious human. Dirt covers her skin, and even though her golden hair shines through the darkness, gorgeous and soft, I can tell it's dirty and matted in certain places. I want to caress the tangles out, but I'm afraid the light will burn.

My seed still drips from her red and raw entrance, but it doesn't seem like I've caused damage. She has minor scrapes and bruises across her delicate flesh, but the most unsettling injury is a cut slashed across her stomach. It's already scabbing, but I can tell it was created since she's been in my possession; the skin is still red and irritated. I kiss the wound, desperate to take away the pain I'm unsure if I inflicted.

She groans, shifting underneath me. I don't stop kissing her, hoping that once she pushes me away, her body will be anew, free of pain. "What are you doing?" she asks, her voice groggy.

I don't look up, just rest a horned side of my face against her abdomen. "Did I do this to you?"

"Do what?"

"This cut?" I sit up, glaring over her, steam leaving my nostrils. "Who did this to you?" I'll kill whoever hurt my Marie, even if it was me.

She sits up on her forearms, her beautiful face scrunched. Sadly, she's still as dirty and beaten as when I began my kisses. She wipes her mouth with the back of her hand, rubs her eyes, and takes in our surroundings before staring down at her stomach, running a hand over the wound. "I got it from pulling myself out of the cage." She chuckles. "Kind of forgot it was there."

I lean over her, cupping her jaw. "So it was me. If I hadn't put you in that cage, you wouldn't be hurt." I want to throw myself off a cliff.

She squints, a humorless smirk at the corner of her rosy lips. "Um, yeah. Also, if you didn't kidnap me at all, I'd be cozy in my bed, vegging out to reality TV shows."

I don't understand half of what she says, but I comprehend the first part. I took her from her safe world and thrust her into my dangerous realm. "I don't remember," I mutter, my gaze downcast.

"Don't remember what?"

"Anything." But it's not true. Nuggets of the past rise to the surface, a warm memory coming first. "Scully," I say through a whisper.

"What?"

"That's my name. I remember now. Scully."

She sits up fully, crossing her legs and studying me curiously. "Scully? Hmm."

I try to dust off the faded picture in my mind. "Yes, someone who cared for me gave it to me a long time ago." I can't make the person out, but it was someone soft and sweet, perhaps someone like my Marie.

Something flashes across her face that I don't register. She shakes her head slightly. "Well, now that your memories are returning, do you remember what just happened?" Her eyebrow arches.

I pull her close to me, even as she keeps her arms crossed over her chest. "Yes, it was the most wonderful moment I've ever experienced."

She scoffs. "You kind of didn't give me a choice and made me pass out."

My heart stops. "You didn't want me, but you clung to me, begged for more?"

Her cheeks bloom a dark red, and she turns away from my stare. "Maybe, I didn't hate it."

I kiss her rosy cheek, working down her neck. "I can give you more." I gently push her to the ground, and she yelps. I crawl over her, kissing her stomach until I'm at her cunt. "I'll lick my seed out of you. I'll make you feel so good you'll heal from all your pain."

Her body shivers, and she breathes heavily, but instead of spreading her legs and welcoming my cock, she pushes my horns away. She exhales, shaking her head. "No. We can't do that right now. I need water, food, and clothes."

I'm embarrassed, a feeling I don't remember. "Of course. I'll bring you back everything you need. You stay here. It's too dangerous out there." I don't give her time to respond, crawling up the walls and out of the hole to quickly find my Marie's necessities.

I didn't want to travel all the way back to my cave. Luckily, I'm able to find a fruit tree nearby. For some unknown reason, I know the meat inside the hard shell is edible for humans. A stream bubbles nearby, and I fill a broken fruit shell with the warm water. I must climb a tall tree to retrieve a few of its long, flat leaves. Perhaps Marie can use these to cover herself instead of the large piece of fabric she hides behind. I don't know why she insists on staying hidden, but it doesn't come as too much of a shock to me. I remember humans do not like to live bare.

I race back to the hole, hating to leave Marie for even a morsel of time. It's like my blood rots when she's not around. Not only that, but the creatures in these woods are dangerous. They are like me before my Marie screamed for me. They would do anything to have her to themselves.

My heart doesn't settle until I've dropped back down and scooped Marie in my arms, running my hand over her back. My paw grazes her hair, and I wince at first—anticipating pain—but it's different now. It doesn't sting as harshly but almost soothes. I want to rub my face in it. "My Marie," I whisper. I return to myself even more with her breath against my neck. She pushes me back, and I can't deny the hurt.

"You're giving me whiplash."

"Whiplash?"

She settles on the floor, the horrid brown fabric over her perfect body, crossing her legs in front of her. "Yeah. One second, you're growling at me, jerking off, and unable to utter more than one word. The next, you're crying over my cut and whispering my name. You're like a little kitten now."

"What is a *kitten*?" I can only hope it's something with a big cock.

She sighs. "It's a tiny, cute animal back in my world."

"I am not tiny."

Her eyes trail down my body, her pupils growing. "Nope, you're definitely not."

Her stare rattles my bones. I enjoy her attention, but she must eat and drink to regain her strength. With her hot gaze on me, the urge to throw her to the ground again is overwhelming. I shrug, ready to build words around our tension. "Well, which version of me would you prefer?" I would do anything for her, even pretend to still be the monster that her cunt cried for moments ago.

Her gemstone eyes grow wide. She doesn't answer, just shakes her beautiful head. "Did you bring me back something?" She must feel the same about the direction of our conversation.

"Yes." I grab the shells from behind me, offering them to her. She accepts them warily, sniffing each before placing them in front of her. "These smell funny. What is it?"

"It's fruit and water from the stream. I don't know how, but I know you can eat and drink them."

"Do *you* eat and drink this?"

I shake my head. "No. I survive on screams."

"Ah, yes. That's right." She gives a forced laugh and takes a small sip of the water. "Eh, it's warm." Her scrunched lips reach her nose.

"You don't like it. I can try to get more from a different section." I stand up, ready to make the trip again, but she stops me. "No, no. It's fine." She downs the entire contents of the shell before moving onto the broken half of the fruit with the green meat inside. She smells it and winces before digging a piece out and bringing it to her lips to eat. "Ugh. That's so gross."

"I can get you something else. I can snap the neck of a howler and feed you its eyeballs. Would you prefer that?"

"No! Don't do that. That's so much worse. Are you sure I can eat this, though?"

I shrug.

"I guess I don't have much of a choice. She winces as she peels off more of the meat inside the fruit shell, gagging after every few bites, but eventually eating all of it. She lies on the ground once she's finished. "I can't eat that for the rest of my life."

I crawl to her, holding myself up over her so I can look into her eyes. "We can find you something else."

Her face is expressionless. "Scully, I need to go back home."

I almost don't register the words after my name—the sound of it on her delicate lips—almost. My black heart aches. "I'm your home now."

"Scully," she says my name so soft and sweet, but even my fresh intelligence can't pretend she means anything I want. "I can't live like this. I will resent you and wither away if you keep me here."

I don't want to scare her. I don't want her to stay with me because I forced her, but I can't help it. Steam leaves my nostrils, and my eyes burn. "You can't go back."

She doesn't retreat at my anger, pressing forward. "Because it's impossible or because you don't want me to?"

"It's impossible." It's a lie. I could take her back to the portal from which I had taken her. I've never done it before, but I don't see why it wouldn't work if she jumped back through. It always takes me to the same room, but I can't let her know that. I can't live without her.

A new feeling washes over me as I watch her brazen demeanor crumble. She pulls her knees to her chest and lets her head fall. For the first time since I've captured her, she cries. I've heard humans cry a thousand times before. It never affected me, but now it's like a claw through the gut. A small part of me wants to give her what she wants and bring her back to her world, but I shove it down. Instead, I use this as a chance to comfort her.

I pull her into me, wrapping her in my arms and running my hand down her golden hair. We'll need to go to the stream soon so she can wash up and we can collect more fruit before we start our journey home, but not until her tears have dried.

Each stroke of her golden locks feels better. I hum. "You feel so good."

"What?" she asks through a whimper.

"Your hair. It used to burn me, just like the light beyond the dark woods, but now it feels good."

She pops up, startling me. "What light beyond the woods?"

"It's a few days' travel, but beyond the canopy of tall trees, light cages us in. If we touch it, we burn."

"Is it sunlight?"

"It's the color of your hair."

She pops to her knees, grabbing my arms. "You have to take me."

I shake my head. "It's dangerous."

"Scully." She cups my jaw, barely because her hands are so tiny. "It's my only hope. If there is sunlight, then maybe there's civilization. Maybe the light keeps away the monsters, and all the humans live on the edge."

"But I'm a monster. I can't go into this *sunlight.*"

"You're different now. You remember your name. You talk. You even said that my hair used to burn you, but now it doesn't. Maybe the sunlight won't burn you either."

She has a good point, but still, the instinct to stay away from the light runs deep. Besides, my home is all I know. I'm not sure if I want my life to be any different. But that's

not true. I want Marie. Marie makes my life different in a good way, and if she needs this *sunlight* to make her happy, it's the least I can do to bring her to it.

I nod. "Okay. I'll bring you to the light."

"You will?" She smiles, all her bright white teeth showing, and sparks in her eyes. It's such a beautiful sight. I make it my mission to look at her happiness for the rest of my days.

"Yes."

"Oh, thank you!" She wraps her arms around me in an embrace, her breasts pressing against my chest.

I can't help it, my cock hardens from underneath, but I know it's not the time to take her again. She needs to recover, but it won't be long before I have her screaming for me again.

Perhaps I still won't be able to enter the light. I just hope I can convince her that a life with me in the darkness, choking around my pleasure, is enough. We'll take the long way to the light, just to be sure.

Chapter 10: Marie

I insisted on walking on my own two feet and yet here I am, slung across Scully's back like an insolent toddler. To be fair to his rather annoying insistence, I'm still sore from running through the woods without stretching, being attacked by a giant lizard, and being fucked sense-less. Not to mention the utter lack of sleep and shortage of calories. I want to seem like a boss ass bitch during the chances I get to counteract my willingness to scream around his cock and beg for him to keep going. I'd never get him to take me somewhere if he knew how desperate

I was for the pleasure he gave me, but I don't even have my fucking mismatched shoes anymore. I'll have to find another time to regain my independence because I sure as hell am not walking through a monster-infested forest barefoot.

I remain rigid for the first ten minutes of the trek, staying vigilant to every twig snap or screech, but then I fade out, burying my head in his fur and clinging to his neck as he walks along. I'm in such a deep sleep that when a loud boom goes off in the distance, I wake with a scream, forgetting where I am.

"Shh!" he orders in a low whisper, pressing me to his chest. "It's just a boomer throwing a fit far away." I want to ask what the fuck a boomer is, but I know it won't help still my racing heart. I'll just pretend it's an old person demanding their expired coupons be honored, like in my world. I'll grab hold of any sense of normalcy my brain can muster

I take in my surroundings, and of course, I squirm in my sudden arousal from my fear of the noise, hoping he doesn't sense it. Luckily, I'm wearing the makeshift undergarments I finagled together with the floppy but sturdy leaves he brought back. Never thought I'd use the origami I learned from state summer camp to make myself undergarments, but it was finally the time to be thankful for the useless skill.

"How did I get into your arms?" I ask once my blood pressure evens.

"You were slipping off my back, so I pulled you to my front."

"Damn, I thought I'd have better survival skills than that. I've never been a hard sleeper."

"You can sleep as soundly as you want with me. I'll keep you safe."

I roll my eyes. I believe him, but it's still pretty ironic coming from the monster who stole me from my bed.

I'm not sure how long I was asleep. Everything looks subtly different now. It's still as dark as ever, but there's more foliage around—odd papery bushes and trees that must not need sunlight to survive. "Where are we?" I ask.

"We're closer to the light now. About two more days' travel."

"I don't know how you can tell. Everything is just dark and depressing."

He shrugs, looking down at me. "It's my home."

"Do you enjoy living here?"

"I haven't enjoyed much in life, at least not that I remember, until I met you." I don't know if he means he is remembering things more since being with me, or if he enjoys things now that he's with me, but I won't let my fluttering heart ask him to clarify.

"Do you remember where you came from? Your parents?" I ask.

He's silent for a moment, as if searching his brain. "I remember someone gave me my name, someone soft and kind, but nothing else. Perhaps more will come back to me." I wonder if he's referring to another woman he kidnapped. Maybe I'm not the first victim to bring back his reasoning. There could have been someone before me who fell for him and even gave him a name. It stings a little. Mainly because there's no human woman here now, so obviously whoever gave him his name had an untimely death. Another small part feels a little jealous, like maybe I'm not special. I stuff the stupid morsel of myself away.

"What about you?" he asks, surprising me.

"I came from Earth. You know, the place you stole me from?" I lay my head back against his muscular yet surprisingly soft biceps, flashing a tight-lipped grin up at him. His golden eyes stay focused on the path before us. He doesn't register the jab, his face remains neutral and he continues with his questions. "What was growing up there like?"

I sigh, allowing myself to get more comfortable in his arms. "I didn't have a normal childhood. I never knew my parents. My birth mom gave me up to the state when I was a baby. Someone had me for the first few years, but then I think something bad happened because I got taken away, and for the rest of my childhood, I bounced around from different foster homes to group homes."

His eyes soften, the brightness dulling. "I do not know what most of your words mean, but it sounds like a hard life for you."

I chuckle. "Yeah. It wasn't easy, but I aged out of the system and was starting to make it on my own. Growing up, most people in my life—for the short time they were there—assumed I'd become an addict and end up in jail, or on the streets. The system loves to recycle." It feels good to tell him all this, although I know he barely understands what I'm saying. Maybe that's what makes it easier.

He sighs. "Your world sounds awful. It's a good thing you're here."

I sit up in his arm, climbing his chest to study his expression. His eyes move to mine, and I catch the mischievous sparkle. I can't help but laugh. "Yeah, thank God I'm here and don't have to work a dead-end job. I just have to live in total darkness, run from monsters trying to kill me, and deal with you."

He tsks, grinning. "I thought I was just a big *kitten*?"

"Yeah, a kitty that stole me, locked me in a cage of human remains, and is constantly trying to rip me in half."

His lips scrunch around his fangs. "I seem to remember you begging me to rip you in half."

I slap his chest, my cheeks heating. "Clearly your memory isn't sharp."

"Maybe if you scream for me some more it will help."

I laugh, throwing myself down in his arms and turning back to the woods before us with my arms over my chest. "You're a menace." Are we flirting? I should *not* be flirting with my captor. Although, everything else I've been willing to do seems like it's more of the issue.

Scully chuckles and a comfortable silence passes over us. I focus on the woods around me to ground myself to reality. Maybe Scully's charming and maybe he makes my body sing like a church choir, but it doesn't mean my situation is any less dire. I sigh. "I'm just ready to get out of these shitty woods and into the light."

He doesn't respond, and his body tenses. I wonder if it's because he's scared of the light, or if I hit a nerve by insulting his home. The tension between us is much worse than the filtration before. For some unexplainable reason, I don't want to hurt his feelings. I also don't want him to second guess his decision of taking me to the light. I search for another topic of discussion and luckily, it comes to me like a sweet bird's song. "Do I hear water?"

He listens for a second, his downcast ears twitching under his horns. "Yeah, there must be a stream nearby."

"Can we go? I desperately need to wash myself."

He nods, turning to the source. "I was going to bring you to the spring near the hole, but you passed out so quickly, and I didn't want to wake you."

I urge my heart to stop swelling. It's the least he can do after running me ragged, but I can't help how I blush and hope that he doesn't notice the hue in the dark. I remain quiet until we're entering a small clearing and steps away from the stream.

Neon green moss illuminates the riverbanks. Clear water rushes over smooth stones. The scene is as tranquil and familiar as a river back home—much darker, but flickering lights provide an ethereal glow. "Are those lightning bugs?" I ask excitedly, pointing to the dancing creatures above the current.

He shrugs, placing me on the ground. "I call them burners, because they burn when they touch you."

I yank back my hand, seconds away from touching the nearby insect. Then I remember that my hair burned him as well and decide to test his words. The burner lands on my finger, just like a lightning bug would, and surprise, surprise, it doesn't burn. I turn to him, presenting my discovery, with a giddy smile.

He shakes his head. "It's because you're full of magic."

Why is he being so goddamn sweet? I'm thankful for the cover of darkness and hope the little guy on my finger doesn't reveal my heated cheeks. I turn toward the water, looking through the flowing translucent surface. "You should touch one. See if they stop hurting you like my hair did." I lower my toe into the water, prepared to lose it if it isn't safe for me. It's better than blushing like a schoolgirl at my captor.

Scully giggles. Fucking giggles, and I whip around. Burners land all around him, and he smiles at one resting on his finger. "They tickle."

I can't help but laugh. It's so preposterous. He's a monster, my kidnapper, my assaulter, and he stands before me, giggling over twinkling bugs. My laughter turns into hysteria. I can't control myself. I throw my head back, losing my balance and slipping on a wet rock near the edge. I splash into the water with a scream, tensing for scalding acid or needling water creatures to assault my skin, but after my initial fright—and of course, the start of arousal—my brain registers the sensation of the cool, refreshing water surrounding me. I'm ready to wade in it, already feeling a million times better, but Scully lunges after me, scooping me up in his monstrous arms and pulling me to his chest, his heart beating like a jackrabbit.

"My Marie, are you okay?" I stare up at him, shocked by the overpowering concern in his glowing eyes. My hands are against his chest, and my fear of falling in and now being pulled out so abruptly can't be ignored. But I'm not afraid of *him* anymore.

His intense stare takes me in. He looks as if he would destroy the world to keep me safe, an expression I've only ever seen in movies, never in real life. I don't want the moment to end. I've always only wanted to care for myself—independence—but now a hollow and empty part of me pangs. Perhaps I want to be protected, to be wanted so desperately that someone would rip a part of the world to get to me, rip apart another monster with his bare hands. Of course, I can rationalize that my scattered psyche as a parentless child growing up in a cold and unloving world could easily make his obsession look like something to be desired instead of feared. Still, maybe I can enjoy it for a moment. I have nothing better to do, and plus, it looks like I'm staying in this realm, whether I like it or not.

My lips nearly collide with his, without questioning how kissing would work around his fangs, but then he's the one to ruin the moment. "Are you okay?" he asks again.

I startle, pulling back, remembering myself. "Yeah. I just fell in. Is it safe for me to be in here?"

"The only place in this world safe for you is hidden in my cave, especially when you scream, but the water won't hurt you." His ears twitch. "And I don't hear any creatures nearby, so I think your scream went unnoticed."

I nod, swallowing and looking away from his piercing eyes. "Okay, good."

"Can I help you bathe?"

"What?"

"Your hair is very tangled. I can release some of the knots with my claws."

I don't want to argue. I don't think I could find the words with my confusing thoughts, so instead I nod. "Okay."

He sets me back down in the water, ripples lapping above my stomach. The cool stream flows calmly, sending my relaxed arms ahead of me. I straighten my legs and fall to my back, floating atop the surface as the water cascades around me. My large coat is entirely drenched, and I need to take it off to get completely clean. I didn't mean to fall into the water, but I don't mind that my only piece of clothing came in with me. It belongs to a dead man after all. It could probably use a little cleaning as well.

I sit up, stripping the heavy fabric off my body. I don't have to turn to Scully to know he's staring at me. Thank God I'm still wearing my leafy wrap-bra and underwear so I don't feel even more vulnerable than I already do. I catch him at the corner of my eye, seated but nearly all of him above the water. He waits patiently, monstrous hands clasped in his lap. It makes me uneasy that he's so calm, so un-monster-like. At least when he was without consciousness, I knew what to expect; now I don't know what side of him I'll get. I wonder if the uncertainty is the cause of my pebbled nipples or if it's the cool water. But of course, I know the answer.

I give the fabric a little rub before wringing it out and laying it over a large stone near the edge. We probably won't stay here for long, so it won't fully dry, but I'm taking it with me, sopping wet or not. Maybe my attempts to dry it won't do much, but it's the least I can do. My gaze snags Scully's as I turn back to the water, taking my seat in the middle of the stream. I hate this godforsaken, spooky-ass forest, but right now, it isn't so bad. Something hoots in the distance, almost like an owl, but with a metallic undertone. The glowing green moss provides a comfortable pocket of illumination. The fireflies, or burners, dance around us, their light reflecting off the water's surface and making it sparkle. They match Scully's eyes. I wonder if he realizes that.

I lay back again. He'll run his claws through my hair soon, but I need to wash it off the best I can first. You'd think I'd have to explain this fact to him, but he remains still, patient as ever. I nearly scream again as the current increases and my leaf undergarments rip off my body. I cover my mouth, sitting up to hide my nakedness. It's a stupid thing to do. He's seen more of me than my primary care physician, but it's instinct, and once I catch his zeroed-in stare, and his mushroom-like cockhead bobbing out of the water, I'm even more embarrassed—and even more turned on.

We're at a standstill, staring at each other, neither of us letting out a breath, but finally, he parts his lips. "Can I brush your hair now?"

I want to say no, because it's clear his intentions to untangle my locks aren't purely innocent, but God, do I want to say yes more than anything.

So I do.

He cracks the stillness like a twig as he wades forward. I turn around, presenting my backside, thankful—or am I—that the water covers my lower half. His breath heats my shoulder as he leans down to whisper in my ear. "Is this okay?" What is he, the consent king now?

I nod, taking in a hard gulp. He starts at the bottom of my hair, holding a strand with one hand and untangling it with the other so it doesn't pull. He's not pressed against me, something that initially disappoints me, but it's for the best. I do actually need my hair brushed if I want to not have to cut out impossible knots later on. It takes a while for him to get through the matting at the ends, hurting slightly, but nothing unbearable. Once his claws meet the base of my scalp, I moan, leaning back into him. Something bumps against my rear, and I squirm, thinking it's a fish.

"Sorry," he says, as if pained, pulling back slightly.

"Oh, no. It's okay." I lean back into him, even as his dick, fully erect, presses against me. He groans softly as he continues to run his claws against my scalp. His filaments reach out for me, not as strong in the current, but a few attach to my ass, searching for my sensitive bits. I'm so relaxed that I can't even be scared of those guys anymore. Besides, I think my body has clued in my brain that even though they're unusual, their otherworldly ability to deliver pleasure overtakes any aversion. I keep lowering, not even realizing that I'm falling back into him. Scully doesn't halt massaging, working on the top of my head as I lie against his muscular chest.

He's not untangling anymore, just scratching my head, slow and sensual. My chest heaves. I have no shame in my hardened nipple, painfully aching out of the water. I feel his gaze on me, my chest, my bare cunt, my parted lips as I labor against the thick air. His claws move lower, down the side of my face, scratching behind my ears, cupping my jaw, running down my neck.

I arch my back, pushing myself more onto his lap. His dick is at the middle of my back, most of his filaments suctioning and pulling me closer. I'm so aroused. I've never felt this way before. Calmness and yearning tangle together, kindling my nerves into flames.

His claws remain at my neck, not moving lower than my collarbone. I don't want to beg. I push my breasts out of the water, wanting him to obey my silent demand, but he doesn't move lower, clearly wanting me to ask for it. Every part of me fights my mouth, not wanting to give in. It won't be the first time I beg for more, but this time feels different. He's not demanding anything, just offering comfort. If I ask him to touch me, there will be no turning back. The thin veil of my fight will rip to threads.

I can't take it anymore. "Please," I whisper, not opening my eyes.

His words come out torturously slow. "Please what?"

He knows damn well what, but I'm too desperate now to play coy. "Touch me," my breathy voice making the words barely audible. I finally open my eyes, catching him staring down at me—ravenous, awestruck. His eyes flick down my chest as his claws graze lower. He travels through the valley of my chest, taking a detour at the ridge of my mound. "Where do you want me to touch you?"

"Everywhere," I say around a moan.

He moves up my breast, circling my nipple. It's so light yet so intense. "Here?"

"Yes. More."

Who knew my few words could be so useful? His other hand travels down my abdomen. I'm wound tight, panting like he's touching much more than he is. After an eternity, he reaches the peak of my cunt, twirling his claw in my curls.

"Please. Touch me. Please." I watch him as his eyes absorb my body, licking his lips. He grinds against me, and his suctions tighten on my back. I'm sure they'll leave marks.

"So needy." His finger travels lower. From my position, lounging against him, head propped up on his chest, I can see as his fingers tease at my seams. His claws detract, leaving padded, paw-like fingers touching my skin. My pussy floats atop the surface, glistening from my arousal. He plays in it, teasing me still. I buck into his hand, needing more.

"Use your words," he says with a growl. "I love it when you beg."

"Touch inside of me. Make me come." I cry, completely lost.

He does as I ask, parting me, stroking up my velvety skin, still so soft it's cruel. "Do you like this?" he asks, barely touching my clit, but sending my nerves ablaze.

"Yes!" I cry, choking on the word.

"It will be so much better with my attachers, pulling you closer to me." So that's what he calls those little guys—attachers. Makes sense.

He presses harder, and I cry out. His other hand, previously on my breast, covers my mouth. "Shhh, little human. The monsters will hear you. They'll want to feast on you. Watch as I play with you. Take a turn. But you're all mine. Only I will make you whimper and scream." His hands are so large that he's able to tease two of his fingers at my entrance while still caressing my clit. I press down on his hand, wanting more, craving release.

His hand falls away from my mouth and returns to my breast, pinching my nipple as he fucks me with his hand and massages my hardened bundle of nerves. I can't suppress the scream. The world falls away. I'm no longer in a forest surrounded by monsters. I cry out as my mind washes blank and my orgasm hits me. He groans along with me, rutting into me until his warm cum jets against my back. "Scream for me, just like that."

He wrings me out, my body raw and my vocal cords strained. It's not until I'm completely sated, my consciousness returning, and my heartbeat slowing that I realize what I've done. Scully tenses, presumably coming to the same conclusion. He tenses, his attachers release me, and he sits up, cradling me against him. Something splashes down the stream, followed by a clicking.

He jumps out of the water, carrying me with him. I nearly scream, but I catch it in my throat. Something jumps out of the water just as we exit. This time, Scully covers my mouth, anticipating my fear. A slimy yellow slug-looking creature snaps its jaw at me, revealing rows of razor-sharp teeth. Its beady eyes are hooded below a jutting forehead, making it look like it's grimacing at me, almost like a bitchy giant worm. Scully backs away as more of it trails out of the water.

"I thought you said the water was safe?" I inquire, not taking my eyes off the massive creature. It moves incredibly slow, and I hope it's not a stalking technique before it pounces.

"It was. I couldn't sense the rozzers when we entered."

I want to argue that if he told me that these "rozzers" were a possible inhabitant of the stream, I'd have taken a quicker dip and not have waded in the water as he took his time with me, but I don't have the chance. A low gurgle comes from deep within the dense woods next to us. I have a feeling my scream alerted a whole bunch of different creatures, much like last time. Scully must have the same idea. He scoops me in his arms and takes off in the way we came, holding me close with one hand, and pushing away tree limbs with the other. I hide in his chest fur, not wanting to look, especially as footsteps and growls follow after us, sporadically growing closer.

After what feels like forever, my entire body and hair nearly dry, Scully slows, his breath barely labored. I pop up. We're in a small clearing. Trees, looking more like Earth trees than the others I've seen, cage us in. A rock formation sits in the middle.

"Where are we?" I ask.

"A cave. It should be safer here but let me check." He drops me to the ground. The gravel grazes my ass, reminding me I'm naked. Shit. I forgot my coat, but it hardly seems like the time to ask to go back.

Scully nears the entrance of the cave. His nose and eyes twitch as he searches around and pokes his head into the darkness.

"How did you know this was here?"

"I've been here before."

"You have?"

"I think I've tried to make this journey before. It's coming back to me."

I want to ask more, but he disappears into the entrance. I look around, noticing some rocks covered in the neon green plants. I pull them off so we can have some lighting when we're inside.

Scully emerges, his frantic eyes finding me. He charges, scooping me back into his arms, and exhales as if he held his breath the entire time we were a part. "It's safe." He buries his nose in my hair and carries me inside.

Immediately, Scully lays me on the ground next to him, pulling me into his arms. I don't push him away. I don't question him more about the creatures that followed us or what he remembers now. I just lie with him, letting his heat warm me, his coat already dry and comfortable.

I'm so at peace, even after being chased. My orgasm is probably the root of my comfort. In fact, it was unlike one I've ever experienced before. Of course, it could be because it was from a monster strumming me in an alien, danger-infested stream, but I wasn't frightened at all.

It hits me. That's it. It was the first orgasm I've ever experienced without being scared. And damn, was it good.

CHAPTER 11: SCULLY

I'm sure I'm in a dream, even as the fog of my slumber disappears. Her heart beats against my palm. Her soft form molds into me. I don't move, even as my cock aches to part her cheeks and enter her—whatever hole she'll allow. I suppress my urges, instead focusing on the even cadence of her breath. I stir slightly so I can get a better look. She's so peaceful, no creases line her face. Her hair is even more golden than when I captured her. It lies in waves around her face—soft and clean. Her skin is unblemished, free of dirt and grime. I'm thankful I took care of her. Not that she needs to be clean for me to want her nearby. Even covered in mud, she'd be beautiful, but I know she prefers it this way.

I can't resist. I gently run my hand over her skin, unbelieving it could be as soft as I remember. Of course, it's even more so. She stirs slightly from my contact but doesn't make any indication of rising. She sighs contentedly and nuzzles closer to me, her ass making contact with my groin. I'm unable to stop myself from growing. I will my attachers to calm. If they came out to play, she'd be up for sure and I want to watch her like this forever—happy and safe in my arms. If the cave fell on me now, I'd die happy. That is, if she made it out alive.

As I watch her, realization washes over me and my happiness fades. I lied to her, told her there was no way to take her back home. At the time, it seemed like the only option. I couldn't live without her, and now it's even more so. But with every scream comes a new layer of myself. It's not just about me or my survival. It's not enough to keep her safe from harm. She deserves to live the life she wants, even if that life isn't with me. What is this feeling?

Love. Of course. I remember it.

My peaceful moment is gone; instead, sorrow. There's only one more day's journey until we reach the edge of the woods, into the light. I must tell her the truth now, and I don't believe the pleasure I've brought her will be enough for her to want to continue, to give up her world for an unknown world for us both. I wouldn't want her to do such a thing, especially for a monster like me.

My Marie yawns, arching her body against me and raising her hands overhead. It hurts, her body is so erotic that it physically pains me—pains my dick that will never know the bliss of her inner walls grasping me again. Once I tell her the truth, she'll never allow me into her sweetness. I'd never take it from her or corner her until she can't resist. I'm different now—a version of myself I actually remember, even if it's been ages.

She turns to me, her eyes barely open but her smile already in full bloom. She rubs her face into my chest, inhaling. I groan, keeping my touch light on her back. "I can't remember the last time I've slept so well, and I'm on a stone floor."

Every time I hear her voice, it's like a balm over the cracked layers of my heart. There's still a selfish part of me, wanting to savor the last moments with her body against mine. I pull her close to me, sniffing her bright hair, saving the curves of her body against mine to memory. It's useless, though. Once she's gone, so are my memories. I'll return to savagery, surviving off screams of terror, never truly sated. I shiver at the thought, but it's worth it. Even as she hums, happily against me, her fingers dancing in my fur, I know it's all an illusion. She's tricked herself into happiness because she thinks she has no other choice.

She trails kisses up my chest. "How long can we stay here?" she asks.

I'm dizzy with lust, but I focus on answering her question. "As long as you'd like. We're only a day away from the light." I don't mention that we might turn back so she can be returned to her world. I'm enjoying her traveling hands too much.

She pulls back, looking up at me, drowning me in her blue eyes. "Why have you been here before? Have you visited the edge?"

I nod, grimacing at the raw memory from so long ago, new in my mind. "My mother brought me."

She sits up, her eyes wide. "You remember your mother?"

I reach out and touch the bottom of her golden locks. "Yes, she had hair like yours."

She pulls her knees into herself, studying me. A small, selfish part of myself hates that I'm talking, making her interested, and covering her bare body from my view. I should be using my newfound language skills to entice her to spread her legs for me, but that small part of me is easily squashed. Her interest is just as riveting to witness. "Yes.

I remember her. She was human and strong like you. She gave me my name and loved me. She wanted us to leave these woods so I could have a better life. We stopped here for a few nights."

"Was it just you and her?"

I shake my head. "I had a father. A monster like me."

"But was he..."

"Mindless? Not with her. He loved her. She gave him his mind like you gave me mine, but I remember it didn't always stay that way. He wasn't always kind to her."

"Did he hurt her?"

"Yes. Many times. I was so young, but I remember it. I lived off her screams from him. She escaped with me, hearing the rumors of the light beyond the woods. But monsters found us and took her from me." I turn away, the memory heavy against my chest. I miss the mother I barely even knew—the mother I lost so long ago, but even more sad is what this memory means for me now. I could be like my father. This self could disappear, even with my Marie near. It's just another confirmation that she should return to her world.

As if reading my mind, she cups my chin, turning me back to her. "You're not him. You're part human. You have humanity in you."

I push her touch away gently. "You don't know me well enough."

"You wouldn't hurt me."

"But I have hurt you. I stole you from your life. I kept you in a cage. I scared you. I forced myself on you. I could do that again."

She grabs my chin again, anger in her eyes this time. "And if you do. I'll scream for you. I'm turned on by fear. If you scare me, it will only make me want you more and I'll bring you back to me. I hated you at first, hated myself for my sick fetish, but I think we're made for each other as crazy as that sounds. You give me what I need and I can do the same for you. We'll get to the light tomorrow and we'll start a new life together."

"No." She blurs in front of me, water in my eyes creating a shield—tears. It's been so long, but I remember them. "That's not all. I lied to you."

"About what?"

"You can return to your home. I could bring you back through the portal, and you'd be back in your room."

Her eyes are heavy. "You lied to me?"

"I'm sorry. Even after you cleared the fog in my mind, I was still less than. All I thought about was myself. I couldn't live without you. I *can't* live without you, but now I care for you as much as myself, not just something to be owned. It's not safe for you here. Even if we were in a place void of mindless monsters, you'd never know when I could revert back to my old self."

Her face remains void of emotion, and silence wades between us. I want to speak more, apologize on my knees, but she deserves to have space to process and lash out at me however she sees fit. She turns away from me. It hurts not being able to study her or predict her following response, but I wait patiently, even if it feels like forever. Finally, she sighs, breaking the silence. "I have gone crazy."

I don't reply.

"I should hate you. I should have always hated you, and yet after everything..." I grab her shoulder, turning her toward me, needing to see her lips as she speaks because I can't believe it. "I understand."

"You do?"

She turns fully. "Of course, it was wrong to kidnap me and lie about it, but you're a monster." Realization washes over her face, and she reaches for me. "You *were* a monster. Now you're just Scully. My Scully."

"But what about your world? You're willing to leave that all behind?"

She shrugs. "I mean, my world is pretty shitty. Not as much as here, but I was always in danger, always struggling. At least here I have you."

I don't move at first, too shocked by her words. Not only is this woman smart, funny, and resilient, but she's also more forgiving than she should be. She spoke of a hard past, one that should have made her wary of others, especially from the likes of me. Yet, she chooses to put it behind her—for me.

I scoop her in my arms, embracing her like she'll fly away if I let her go. "I don't deserve you." I whisper.

She laughs, pushing back. "I know. What can I say? Maybe your monster cock fucked the sense out of me."

I laugh, because I can tell by her smile that she's joking. I run a paw down her arm. "Just promise me, if the light isn't what we hope, you'll consider going back to your world."

"But..."

I tilt her chin toward me. "Promise you'll consider."

Her expression sobers. She nods and I pull her back into me. She nuzzles into my fur, wrapping her arms around my neck, and I stroke her back.

Perhaps I was right earlier—I am in a dream. It seems like the only possible conclusion. She straddles me and after a moment of stillness she slightly pushes herself against me, signaling her desire.

My cock reacts first, hardening and meeting her lips. She moans, grinding against my length.

I don't deserve her—an understatement. And I definitely don't deserve her screams after my confession. Yet, as I think about her reaction and willingness to leave everything behind just from knowing me for a short time, I wonder if her screams aren't only for me. Perhaps the release heals a broken part of her as well.

Chapter 12: Webs

I followed them here, thankful to encounter a scream that cleared my mind enough to focus on staying hidden. I've always been stealthy, quiet steps and breaths that turn my prey into unsuspecting victims. Capturing her alone would have been easy, but the male has instincts to protect what's his. I almost beat him and got her for myself, but he's stronger than me, even more so now. I had to recover from our fight, gain more strength, and come up with a plan as I trailed them through the woods.

I'm perched on the top of the cave—my eight appendages make it easy to remain at an awkward angle and peek into the small opening at the top. It's dark inside, but a soft glow from the plants she brought in with her illuminates the space.

I need to hear her scream again. Surely, he's still more lethal than I am from her being so near while she howls. It's not just the screams, though. I've watched them. He wrings pleasure from her, eliciting a response I've never experienced, one that makes me pop from my hard casing, taking myself in my claw until I release. That alone has brought me power, but surely it would be even more if she rode me like she does him, screaming for *me*.

Excitement coursed through my veins when they both awoke from their slumber. I was eager for them to perform for me, to listen to their wet noises, the moans, and most delicious—her screams. But they spent time talking to each other—flapping their fleshy mouths as their faces contorted around emotions. My rage at their stalling almost made me burst in through the opening and fling her over my shoulder, but that would have been foolish. Even sneaking up by surprise wouldn't grant me victory. I had to get her alone, of course, but my need for their coupling almost became too much. I'm growing impatient as the darkness creeps over my mind, making me return to my starved state.

Somehow, he can last longer than I. He can reason for even longer periods between her screams. I can only assume it's due to his member entering her, squelching inside as he releases. Soon it will be my turn, but for now, I watch, eager to see them in the act.

She's been naked their whole slumber and conversation. It drives me senseless that he can sit before her in such a state, without forcing her mouth to his heat. I would not be able to hold so much reserve. Perhaps he allows her reprieve to elicit a great response from her later. Surely, I've noticed the difference between her screams of pleasure compared to the ones I usually gather from terror. I'm thankful for the haired beast, even if I yearn to yank out his heart and steal his prize. If it weren't for him, I'd be clueless about how to squeeze the sweetest nectar from her fruit. I'd squander and run her dry. He must feed the female and bathe her. I'm hopeful that I can remember to do these things when she's in my possession.

I haven't come up with a plan yet. Every scream, I'm more capable, and I hope that this next one will give me the mental power to overtake them both. Right as my vision blurs with red and my last ounces of reserve dwindles, the female throws her arms around him, her bare sex atop his. They're tender at first, something that does nothing for me, but then she begins to move atop him, pivoting her hips in slow movements. The thin sticky members encircling his length creep from underneath him, and all I can make out is them worming their way up from behind, suctioning her to him.

She pulls away from his neck, throwing her head back with a moan as he glares down at her full and bouncing breasts. He lowers his head, his long tongue lapping her nipples as if they procure the droplets of terror. I can't wait to have my taste. She grabs onto his horns as she moves her hips over him, her moans growing louder. I don't believe he's penetrated her yet. He's large and would need to lift her up to enter her.

I pull my many eyes away from the opening to look down at my manhood, longer than his but more slender. I retract my casing over one of my appendages so I won't scrape myself. In my armor's place is my soft claw. It won't entirely close around my member, but as long as I'm watching these two, the desire will boil over into release. I'll spill much quicker when I'm inside her. I've witnessed how tight her holes are. Even her mouth would be minuscule in comparison to my girth. I plan to enter her at every orifice until her pores leak with my seed.

Slickness drips from my tip, and I lather my fleshy claw over it, pulling down my length to lubricate myself. I shudder at the sensation of my first yank. It's already mind-numbing. Surely the anticipation has made it all the sweeter. Both of their cries of pleasure draw my attention back into the cave, but I don't release myself. I slow my strokes as I watch, imagining myself raising her up, and slowly impaling her onto me as she begs for more. His skinny members and arm muscles strain as he holds her over him. At the sight, my webbing shoots out from my body, encasing my hand and resisting against the tug to pull up and down. The barrier only makes me harder, closer to my edge—imagining her completely covered in my webbing, unable to move as I move into her, more violent with each thrust.

"Please!" she cries. "Please." She's so desperate for him. It amazes me that he's able to withstand shoving into her. The width of his cock doubles mine. The first time, I was sure she'd split in two, yet here she is—whole and begging for more. He lowers her gently, and I suppress my groan. I want to yell down at them to hurry it up, to impale her on his cock so my mind can piece together what it would feel like to have her all my own. But of course, I'm only growing stronger, and my newfound reason won't let me do such a thing.

I'm enjoying their position. As he delicately lowers her onto him, I have the perfect angle. Her pouty lips are parted, and her breath is so thick I almost feel it. Her breasts jiggle with each shallow thrust he gives. I even notice how his tight strings of skin hold onto the top of her cunt and between her cheeks. They strain each time he pulls away from her before inserting into her again. There's so much liquid already—the sound of it bringing me close to my edge. Once he releases inside of her, she'll leak with his seed. The last few times, I had to stop myself from barging in and drinking his release straight from her opening. There had never been a reason for me to do that before, but I can nearly taste their arousal mixed together on my tongue, and I'm eager to know the true flavor.

He's losing his restraint, pounding into her quicker, and screams bubble at the back of her elongated throat. My eyelids grow heavy, but I will all five of them to stay open. I must watch as she meets her crescendo, crying out in pure pleasure as I release just to have power replaced in my veins.

The scream rises in volume, and I soak it in, my muscles hardening, my vision focusing, and my brain clearing of an ancient fog. Just as he roars, shuddering as he bursts inside of her, I release, my seed coming up in wet webs that stick to my claw and the cave wall in front of me. They'll melt soon, but as I catch my breath and watch the two down below, I'm in no rush to pull away from my own release. I have time. My plan is fully formed in my mind, but I can't move until they're right where I need them to be.

CHAPTER 13: MARIE

It's dark when I wake, because duh, it's always dark. I'm unaware of whether hours or days have passed inside this cave. In fact, I have no idea how long it's been since I was back in my shitty apartment, in the human realm. Perhaps that's why I've found myself so tightly entangled with my monster captor—both figuratively and literally. It feels like a lifetime together, but could also only be a few days.

Scully spoons me, his arms wrapped around my middle, pulling me close. I almost snuggle into him, just like

I've done the last two times after opening my eyes, but it always ends the same way—riding him and falling back into a deep slumber. I blame the highs and lows of my captivity and journey over the last few days. In reality, the world-shattering orgasms causing me to scream, cry, and convulse with pleasure are probably the sole reason for my exhaustion.

I wiggle out from under the muscles and fur, not rising to my feet once I'm free. I watch him for a moment, sleeping peacefully. I try to remember what he looked like when I hated him, but the monster curled up next to me is nothing like the beast that stole me from my room. Sure, he looks the same. He was always handsome in a terrifying type of way—his muscular form, his piercing eyes, his strong jaw, even the horns did it for me. He's unlike anything I've ever seen before, but there's always been an attractiveness to him. Now, staring down at him, he's completely devastating. Maybe it's my brain playing tricks on me, viewing him with a filter since he's rearranged my organs and the shattered pieces of my soul, but whatever the reason may be, I can't deny the intense arousal that washes over me whenever I look at him.

I pull my knees up to my chest, taking the silent moment to gather my thoughts. He lied to me. It wasn't the worst thing he's done in my captivity, and yet it holds a great implication for my future. I've found myself falling off a never-ending cliff—my heart making room for him on the way down. Trauma bonding is real, and I welcomed the Stockholm syndrome theory with open arms when it felt like I had no other choice but to make the best of my shitty situation. The truth makes everything different now. I don't have to stay here. Yesterday (or whenever it was), I told him that I wanted to be with him in the light. He made me promise that if it weren't what we wished for, I'd consider going home. I'm doing that now. Of course, it's hard to do when the hope of a glittery city beyond the gloom still exists in my mind, but I try to visualize the very possible reality that it's just a different form of nightmares, maybe one Scully can't come along to.

Would I have him return me home? The idea no longer appeals to me as it did a few days ago. I shake my head, carefully standing up and walking toward a small passage-way at the back of the cave. Scully doesn't want me to venture outside on my own, and I don't blame him. Luckily, there's a small corridor in the back where I can relieve myself in privacy. I take care of my business, my mind whirling with movies and books I scoffed at throughout my lifetime. I used to hate when the main character would give up her entire life to shack up with some dude she just met. It seemed so unrealistic to me, especially as someone who knows just how deceiving people can be behind a pretty facade.

Now that I'm in my own dark fantasy, the appeal to stay overwhelms my reason, urging me to leave everything behind to be with someone who brings me happiness. Scully never gave me anything but the harsh reality of himself. I've seen him at his worst, and sure, it terrified me, but I'm a sick fuck. I like to be scared. It's not only that. He's given me pleasure without the fear—something previously foreign to me. Perhaps I just want to be wanted and safe for the first time in my life, and Scully offers that in his own strange way, but it wasn't like my life was anything to brag about back home. Sure, I'd felt like I was finally on the brink of leaving my shitty situation and on the pathway to success, but it would have been a challenging climb—one I'd have to do completely by myself for who knows how long.

As I walk back to my sleeping monster, I understand that I could be rationalizing my current feelings because I desperately need a break from the chaos of my real life. This shit could seriously suck in a few weeks once I'm rested and bored, and my only companion in the whole realm is an unpredictable monster. But I guess there's no need to make up my mind now. We'll just have to see what happens when we reach the light tomorrow.

I sit back on the floor, and once I do, Scully's piercing eyes flutter open. He groans and reaches for me. "I missed you."

"I just went pee."

"Too long."

I heed his tugging and roll back into his arms. He sniffs my head as I melt into his warm chest. "Would you rather have me pee right here?" I ask through a smile.

"Yes."

"Ew!" I push him back, but he cages me in.

His chest rumbles with a laugh. "I love everything about you."

My heart hammers. His words are too close to something I don't want to dive into, but I carry on with our banter anyway. "Please don't have a urination kink. I'd think that would ruin everything."

"What is kink?"

"It's like enjoying something out of the norm."

He shrugs, closing his eyes and revealing his fangs with a smile. "If it has to do with you, I enjoy it. I have a Marie kink."

I shake my head against him, glad he can't see my beet-red cheeks.

My stomach rumbles, and Scully pulls back, his eyes searching me as if I just coughed up blood. "My Marie. You're hungry."

I try to remember the last time I ate. Scully got me some fruit just after we arrived. It could have been that I was getting used to their flavor, or that I'd been so properly fucked that even my taste buds were delirious, but the fruit didn't taste as bad as it did last time I ate it. Perhaps it was the fact that we were getting closer to the light—a place where life could be enjoyed—but I try to hold back my ambitious hopefulness.

"I guess I could use something to eat," I say, noticing that my throat is parched as well. My mouth doesn't salivate at the anticipation of the monster coconuts on my tongue, but I can't deny that they seem to be a great form of sustenance. Earth coconuts wouldn't give a human enough calories to last a whole day on their own without making a person feel lethargic and weak. Despite an overall soreness—primarily due to monster dick—I feel pretty good. I'm thankful for the fruit, but I still hope it's not the only thing I have to eat for the rest of my life.

Scully sits up. "I'll go find you something and be right back."

The loss of his heat pains me. I want to pull him back and cuddle up again, but he's right. I can't become so obsessed that I starve. "Okay, but don't be long."

He cups my chin, staring deep into my eyes. "I'll return as fast as I can, and after you eat and drink, I'll fill you with my cock so your screams can strengthen me even more and carry us onward."

I roll my eyes, even as my body flushes from his words. "Okay, whatever."

A part of me doesn't want him to gain more strength and carry me to the light faster. If we prolong the inevitable, we can pretend we'll have a happily ever after—one that isn't guaranteed right now.

He charges toward the cave's exit, ducking as he gets closer. After we arrived, we pulled stones in front of the opening, muffling our noises and keeping us safe. I don't doubt that Scully can take whatever beast tried to attack us, but I felt better that we had a barrier that would give us a head start if someone entered when we were a little preoccupied, which we were...a lot.

He gives me one last longing look before shoving the large rocks to the side and ducking through the opening, stepping outside. I sigh, missing him already. It's ridiculous, but the truth. Just before I get comfortable on the floor and rest until he comes back, something heavy whacks against the ground outside, and Scully roars.

"Scully?" I cry out, but he doesn't respond; instead, he continues to cry out.

My instincts take over, and I rush out of the cave and into the clearing. Scully swings before me, covered in a web netting and hanging from a tree. "Go back inside!" he roars, but it's too late. Something shoots and lands around my ankles, knocking me off my feet and into a dizzying darkness.

CHAPTER 14: MARIE

"This will be pointless if she's asleep." The words are a whisper, growing louder with each syllable. Pain is the first sense that comes to me, new and throbbing. Scully's roar comes next, shaking away any remnants of unconsciousness. The forest around me pieces together, hard to gather at first due to the incessant darkness. Finally, it's obvious. Scully hangs before me, hands tied overhead from a tree, eyes red, fangs revealed, tail slicing the air behind him, and his muscles ripple as he thrashes. Tight binds around my ankles and wrists constrict me, and I look up and down to see that I'm naked and in the same weblike prison as Scully. If he can't get out, there's no point in flailing, but instinct begs me to at least try.

"Ah, there we go. Good job. You've woken the sunray." The monster that's a mix of spider, crab, and pure nightmare crawls in front of my line of vision. I remember him from before, when he attacked Scully to have me for himself. He's not a kind of creature you'd forget—covered in a hard gray shell, eight razor-sharp legs which he switches to use as hands, and five beady eyes twirling in all directions at once. He smiles with his tiny rows of fangs, and fear makes its way through my system. Turns out, I'm not cured. I groan, looking away from the monster before me, hating myself and the godforsaken moisture pooling between my legs.

The spider sniffs and gives a deep-throated growl. "It's not just you. She's ripe for any of us. That will make this so much easier." He reaches out and caresses my jaw.

I gasp, horror surely strewn upon my face, searching for Scully. "No!" I shout, hoping he knows the truth. I only want him, and I can't help my fucked up biology.

Steam bellows from Scully's nostrils, and he thrashes rapidly, the large tree behind him shaking. The spider turns away from me and crawls to Scully. "I knew there was something different about her screams. She's special, and you were keeping her all for yourself." He tsks. "I was going to offer to share her, but then I heard you speaking of bringing her back to her realm and knew you'd gone mad. You'll be useless to me if you can't help me keep her contained."

"I'll kill you!" Scully roars, fighting against the webs.

The spider laughs. "Not trapped in my web, you won't. I should thank you, really. Without your performances every five minutes, I wouldn't have broken through the mental fog and found so much strength. My webs have never been stronger, and I can't wait to see what they'll do when I shoot them inside our pretty little pet until she's bloated with my offspring." His words are horrifying, and my stomach churns with bile. He's been watching us while we had sex, growing stronger off my screams.

"Marie is mine!" Scully roars, shaking the tree behind him even more. The webbing he's hanging from goes so high up that I can't see where he's attached. I look up and see the same for myself. Maybe if this spider angers him enough, he can break free.

"I'll never scream for you!" I yell, whipping the spider's five-eyed attention back to me. "You can chain me and torture me, but I'll never scream, and your brain and strength will wither until you don't even remember why you have me." My words don't shake. I mean it. I've lived through pain, through abuse. Perhaps I'll cry, but he'll never catch a scream from my throat.

He approaches me with a daggered smile. He sniffs the air, the two black holes above his teeth moving upward. "Writhe your legs together all you'd like. You can't hide your sweet smell. I'll have you screaming for pleasure before I even spread your legs." He chuckles and turns back to Scully.

"Fuck you!" I scream, struggling against the webs, growing tighter around my wrists with each harsh movement. I don't care, though. I hope my hands rip from my body so I can show this prick just how much I will suppress my screams.

He ignores me. "Now it's time to kill your preferred monster—preferred at least for now. I don't want you holding onto any hope that he'll save you. It should be easy for me, thanks to your screams." He brings a claw to Scully's furry throat, watching me.

"Wait! No!" My anger calms. "I'll scream for you, just don't kill him. Keep him alive, and you can have me, but kill him, and you'll kill me. What's the point in my lifeless body?"

His face contorts, almost something like confusion. Of course, Scully won't let the spider take me while he's alive.

It's a stupid plan, but I just hope the spider hasn't gained enough reason to realize this.

"Marie, no," Scully says above the claw to his throat, defeat written across his features. *But I have no choice*, I want to yell.

The spider scoffs. "No. I think I'll kill him. I'd rather the fight be gone from you." He pulls back, ready to strike.

"No, I love him!" I yell, my words not registering, panic taking over my senses.

It happens so fast, Scully's eyes shift back to gold, the brightest I've ever seen. He seems to grow before my eyes, changing into something completely foreign. The spider must notice the difference because he pauses—a stupid thing to do, because Scully yanks the webbing, his arms moving like he's yielding a hammer. A giant tree branch falls from the sky, causing the ground to shake upon contact. "Mine!" he yells.

I'm stunned. The spider must be as well because he hesitates. Scully is pure animal, ripping his arms from the webbing the moment his feet touch the earth. He charges the grey beast, knocking him to the ground with a heavy thud.

The last fight between these two was fair, and I was unsure who would win. This time it's different. Yes, the spider may be stronger than before, but Scully doesn't pause. His movements are swift, as if every motion is a pre-planned attack. The spider can barely lift his claws to protect himself before Scully slices his eyes with one clawed hand and with the other rips through the exoskeleton over his chest like it's made of eggshells. He yanks out soft pink innards, red blood splattering across his face and chest. Scully brings the spider's still pulsing muscle to his mouth, taking a bite before tossing the rest of the chunk to the ground beside him. He roars, louder than I've ever heard him before, shaking the universe around us. The world stills. The spider is unmoving underneath Scully's body, his head lolled to the side, his five bloodied eyes shut. Scully swallows before releasing heavy breaths.

I told Scully that I wasn't scared of him anymore. I knew he wouldn't hurt me, and if he reverted to the monster who captured me, I'd scream for him and bring him back from the darkness. But when his blazing eyes whip toward mine and he groans—clenching red-stained fists before stalking toward me, tail raised and waving behind him—absolute terror swims through my veins. He's different; the kitty from before is gone. I can't even be happy that he's alive and that our threat is slain. All I feel is fear—a pulsing, overpowering wave of terror. Which, of course, causes every one of my nerve endings to light.

No, I'm not cured. Maybe I'm worse, because as the monster stalks toward me, bloodied and growling low in his throat, I welcome the fear, eager for how he'll devour me.

He slows as he gets closer, the anticipation building. "Scully? Are you okay?" I ask, my voice shaking.

His eyes are crazed as he reaches me, studying my body as he grabs the web overhead and uses it to support himself. He breathes me in, moaning. "You smell so good. You're marinating for me, growing richer with each second."

I close my eyes, turning my head as he presses his forehead against my cheek. My chest heaves, and I try to stay focused. The spider guy is likely dead, I'm not sure, but he's the least of our worries now. These woods are riddled with monsters, and if he takes me right here there's no way I'll be able to hold back my screams. "Scully, you need to get me out of here." His hand palms my mouth. The coppery taste of blood meets my taste buds. Surely I'm covered in it with his hands all over me and his fangs at my ear. "Shhh, that's not what you want. Your wet little cunt is whispering to me, begging me to take you." With his other paw, he grabs my pussy, slipping his declawed fingers inside of me.

I yelp, and he pushes down on my mouth harder. "Don't call more monsters over. My appetite can't afford more meat that isn't you." He inserts another finger inside of me. I'm so wet that the squelching sound echoes all around us, turning me on even more, but somehow a small part of me stays focused. I free my lips from his hand. "Scully, if you do that, I'll scream."

He inserts another finger, fucking me forcefully. "You think you can be splayed for me like this, dripping with your nectar, spilling words of your love from your lips, and I would be able to last another second without my cock inside of you? No. I will have you now. If you must scream, do it. I can take whatever beast comes our way with your scent covering me." I wonder if my last scream gave him more confidence in his abilities, or if he's too delirious with arousal to think straight. Either way, it's too late for either of us to reason. If he stops, I might die.

He fucks me hard, his fingers reaching deep. "Tell me. Do you want me to stop? Say the word and I'll do it."

"No," I wail, my reason gone, and the only sense in my body is the overwhelming pleasure as Scully works me with his bloody hand. Somehow, he also applies pressure to my clit, and I'm done for. He must sense it as my body tenses, because he presses down on my mouth, muffling my scream. It's still audible, and Scully tilts his horn to my mouth as if trying to catch the fragments that make it through his barrier. He moans and his cock nudges me, his attachers reaching from me.

He doesn't even let me come down from my orgasm as he pushes away. "I can't wait any longer. I have to fill you with my seed." He extracts his claws and swipes against the webbing that holds me up. I yelp as I'm weightless, sure I'll crash against the earth without warning, but his arms swoop around me before I hit the ground, laying me below him as he looms above. He runs his rough tongue over my ear, down my neck, through the valley of my breasts. I look down as he nips at my nipples, being more rough than usual. Sure enough, I'm covered in the monster's blood, and when I pick up my head to look over Scully's massive form, I catch the still unmoving body of the spider monster, not even a hundred feet away. I'm about to get fucked next to a potentially dead body, covered in his blood. The thought should repulse me, dry me up, but instead—because I'm a sick freak—it's like my previous orgasm never happened. My body vibrates in violent anticipation, and if Scully doesn't impale me on his cock quickly, I'll find the power within me to make him.

"Please fuck me. I can't wait." I beg.

Scully pulls away from my breasts and travels back to my ear. "I love it when you beg. Almost as much as I love you." I barely register his words, but it still hits my heart like a bullet, warming me from the inside, even if I don't have the wherewithal to contemplate the seriousness of it. He positions his head at my entrance, already opening for him, ready to rearrange myself to fit around him. His attachers suck onto me, hitting my clit and my back hole with such accuracy it's like they've learned my body.

Scully doesn't even brace himself. I don't think he can. He thrusts inside of me—swift and abrupt, nearly breaking me in half. I cry out—partially due to the pain but mostly from the pleasure. Scully doesn't catch it quick enough this time, but still covers my mouth with his bloodied paw. "We're going to have to run quick after my knot releases. You love calling the other monsters. I bet you enjoy watching me rip through their chest to protect you."

I can't respond. Words wouldn't even know how to make it off my lips. My body and mind are mush as he thrusts into me without caution, without holding back. Thank God he covered my mouth because before I know it, I'm screaming, my insides caving in on themselves. He roars, soaking in my cries as he bursts inside of me, filling me and pooling around my ass. His knot inflates and stretches my entrance wider. His attachers don't let up, and I don't know how it's possible, but I'm coming again, quieter against his hand this time.

Scully falls on top of me, not entirely, or I'd be crushed, but enough to make me feel protected. Our hearts beat against each other, and I'm so thankful for it. To think, just moments before, I wondered if it would be the end of him. Now here we are—fucked silly and catching our breaths—our lips still tingling from the secret words we spoke out loud. I want to say it again, see if it sticks this time, but howls sound from the distance.

The noise knocks Scully out of his trance, and he pushes himself up, his cock popping out of me and spilling the rest of him onto the ground. He still wasn't fully deflated and we both wince in pain. He nearly knocks the air from my lungs as he scoops me up and charges through the woods, away from the monsters.

Chapter 15: Scully

I carried us through the woods all through the night. Marie quickly fell asleep in my arms, and I didn't wake her until I discovered a small stream a short distance from the roughgraveled path. I wanted to keep going until we reached the light, feeling more fearful now than ever before. It took longer than I hoped as I kept getting distracted, staring down at my beautiful Marie as she slept. I'd almost lost her. My life wouldn't be of consequence, but if I were gone while she was trapped in this place, there would be no hope for her. She's so fragile, and a part of me thinks she's right. I'm different   from the other monsters here. I had a human mother who loved me, and although I forgot her for most of my life, she is still a part of me. Thanks to Marie, that hidden piece of myself is back. I wish I could keep it forever, but if it must leave to keep her safe forever, I'd give it up over and over again.

I pause at the river bend, listening for sounds of creatures nearby. "Marie," I whisper when I'm sure it's safe, but of course, it's never safe. Her eyes flutter open, and she sits up in my arms. "Where are we?" she asks.

"We're at a stream. I wanted to clean you off before we kept going."

She studies me, reaching to caress my face. "Are you hurt?" she asks, and it's not the first time. She repeated the question many times before she fell asleep. I didn't answer it at first, too busy running while glancing over every perfect inch of her. She didn't calm or settle into slumber until I responded and told her I was more than fine as long as she was in my arms and safe.

"Yes," I answer. "I just can't keep glancing down to find you covered in blood." I know it's not her own, that it belongs to the monster that threatened us, but I can't help the tightening of my ribs around my heart whenever I glance at her.

"Oh, right," she says, examining herself, but brings her eyes back to mine. "You should clean off, too. The only reason I'm covered in blood is because you are."

I hadn't even thought about it. Haven't thought about myself much at all. I nod. "Let me grab you some food while you're washing, and then I'll wash while you eat." I set her on the ground.

"You won't join me?" Her expression is wounded, and I almost forget my attempts to feed her and pull her into the cool water with me, but I'm more myself now, not clouded by my animalistic urges. That's not true. I want to fuck her more than I want to breathe. I don't think that will ever go away, no matter how many times she screams for me, but now her safety trumps anything else. If we let ourselves get carried away, it can only mean danger, and I must get her out of these woods as soon as possible, even if I can't go with her.

I shake my head, looking away from her eyes. "No, we need to keep moving. It's not safe." I point to the tall tree by the riverbank. "I'll just be right up here so I can watch you."

"Okay," she replies meekly.

"Just don't scream."

She rolls her eyes. "Obviously." She turns toward the water, stepping in but slipping on a wet rock. She gives a little screech but catches herself on both feet. She covers her mouth and turns to me, eyes wide.

I listen again; still, no movement nearby. "We're good."

"Okay, now I promise I won't scream." She pulls down her hand to reveal a smile, and it takes everything in me not to lick it off her face. I watch for a moment, stilling my anxious nerves to convince myself to scale the tree. It's not until after she lies back in the water, floating on the surface, and sits back up to run her hands over her body that I gain the confidence to leave the bank. I've never climbed a tree so fast in my life, and once again, I'm thankful Marie's scream brought me so much strength. I grab two of the circular brown fruit and four large leaves for her clothing, and tuck them under my armpit, falling to the ground with a heavy bang.

"Holy shit!" Marie yells.

"What's wrong?" I ask, rushing toward her.

"You scared me."

My heart settles, registering that my jump may have been louder than she anticipated. I catch my breath, walking toward the bank, dropping the leaves, and cracking open one of the fruits on a stone. "What's new?"

She giggles, falling to her back and floating. "You don't usually scare me."

It's funny. She was terrified of me mere hours ago after I ripped through the monster's flesh and pounced on her as if she were next. Even then, in my animalistic craze, I was still myself—my new, uncovered self. I would never hurt her, and I think a part of her knew that. But still, every morsel of her body shuddered in terror as if I was back to the monster in the dark corner of her room. She wanted the fear. I recognized her subtle reactions so well, and it took such a short amount of time to learn. Perhaps that explains the strong, abrupt need I feel for her—the words that slipped from my mouth as I took her on the forest floor. We're made for each other, even if in the end we discover we can never be.

I contemplate pointing out the recent history of her fright, but I can tell she would rather play this game and I'm happy to oblige. I pour the liquid into one half of the fruit and enter the water, presenting it to her. "Why am I slightly offended?" I offer her the hairy brown shell, and she accepts with a laugh. "You want me to be scared of you?"

I shrug, trying to ignore the way her breasts look covered in the gleam of the water and fall to my back, strategically hiding my budding erection with my thighs. "Sometimes."

"Like when?" She slurps the juice inside the fruit, barely twisting her face in disgust before peeling a piece of the green meat off and slipping it into her plump lips. Everything she does is intoxicating. How can I expect to keep her alive when all I want to do in her presence is fill her?

I dunk myself under the water to cool myself off. "When I'm fucking you." I don't look at her. These words should not be leaving my lips right now. There's only one way they could end, and it does not keep her safe.

She places her partially-eaten fruit half on the surface of the water and swims toward me, her eyes full of desire and her lips below the surface. I tense, anticipating her touch, knowing I won't find the strength to refuse. She rests her top half on my stomach as I float. "Why would you want me to be scared when you're fucking me, hmm?"

I gulp. "Because you gush for me and your screams pierce my soul."

She crawls closer to my lips. "I'm pretty sure I can get just as wet and scream just as loud when I'm not scared. You definitely proved that for both of us, but want to test the theory?"

I don't respond; instead, I let my head roll back. Her hands reach between my legs, finding my cock, hard as stone and standing to attention. She palms my tip, lathering herself in my liquid before slowly rolling down my length. My attachers come to life, reaching for her and suctioning onto her hand. She doesn't let their force deter her; instead, she continues to roll her palm up and down. She can't reach her fingers around me, but the sensation is more than enough, nearly causing me to burst already.

She increases her speed, and I'm completely lost, but then she moans, her head resting on my chest, watching as she strokes me. "Wait," I say, ducking my lower half into the water and sitting up. My attachers heed my mental command and release her.

"What?" she asks, hurt and confusion in her eyes. "Did I do something wrong?"

I scoop her in my arms, staring into her eyes. "Never. You're perfect, always. That's the problem. It's too good, and I'm mere hair-widths away from pulling you onto my lap and filling you until you're leaking with my seed from every orifice. We're nearly to the light. We have to wait."

She gulps, resting a hand on my chest to steady herself. "Why must you say shit like that?"

"Like what?"

"You want me leaking from every orifice? How do you expect me not to jump your bones after you said a thing like that?" She covers her eyes with the back of her hand. I chuckle and throw her over my shoulder, satisfied with both of our cleanliness. I pick up both halves of the fruit,

the uncracked one, and the leaves I gathered for her clothing as she settles herself in my arms. "Ready to reach the
light?" I ask.

"Ready," she replies, but I don't miss the dull look in her
eyes.

There's so much we haven't talked about yet. We don't
know what we'll do if the light isn't what we hoped for or
if she decides the human world is the only place for her. It
would be the right choice, of course, because she can't live
in this darkness, even with me by her side. From my newly
excavated memories, I know sometimes love isn't enough.

CHAPTER 16: MARIE

I've slept enough over the last couple of days to last a lifetime. Of course, I needed it. From fucking to fighting for our lives, my system hasn't worked so long in probably ever. Scully raced through the woods. Not necessarily running, but taking such quick strides that wind pinned me against his chest. Since I napped for almost the entire journey to the end of the woods, I've barely had time to notice, but now I take in the differences. The trees are shorter, and there's no source of light to be found, but the darkness lowers a hue. The path is more defined—still riddled with fallen leaves, branches, and twisting roots, but it appears to lead somewhere. I trust Scully knows the way, and even if the light isn't what we hoped, it's apparent we'll find something at the end of this journey.

"We're almost there," Scully says in a joyless tone, confirming my suspicions of our proximity to the end. I want to question how he can tell, but the darkness fading reveals the answer, each step brighter.

Scully slows, perhaps out of fear of the light itself or for what it will mean for us when we reach our destination. There's a drop up ahead. The woods have been nothing but flat plains, so this change seems important. I can't see beyond the low-lying treetops, and anticipation rings around us, buzzing with speculation about what could be on the other side.

Scully approaches slowly, placing me on the ground once we meet the edge. I straighten out my leafy garments, which are not as structured this time, since I had to craft them on the go, but at least they cover my goodies. I don't want to show up in a brand new place with my tits hanging out. If anything positive can be assumed, it's probably a desert or an uninhabitable forest with sunshine. But on the off chance that people or other people-like creatures are involved, I'd like to be clothed. Scully's mother wanted to come here. There had to be rumors of something good for her to risk her own life and that of her child. Or maybe she was like me, risking it all for hope and love.

He doesn't move, and I can't wait any longer. I step forward, peering over the edge. It's not an endless drop, but a gradual slope. Light shines through an opening at the base, and trees curve around the cleared exit. I take a step closer, eager to peek at what's on the other side. Scully grabs my hand, pulling me back, twirling me to his chest. I stare up at his golden eyes, dimmed with a muted sadness. He doesn't speak, just stares down at me, studying me intently.

"What's wrong?" I ask.

"I just want more time."

I place my hands on his chest. "We'll have all the time in the world once we're on the other side."

He shakes his head. "The light, it could burn me. I might not be able to go."

I shrug casually. "Then we won't go." I look away from his eyes, unable to hold their gaze. It's a mystery that with eyes like his—bright as the sun itself— he can't be in the light. I refuse to believe it.

He pinches my chin, turning me back to him. "Marie."

I push him, an unmovable wall. "Stop. It will be okay. Your mother wanted to bring you here."

"No one knows what's beyond the woods. She was led by hope alone."

"Maybe you're forgetting the truth. Maybe she did know."

He sighs, stepping away from me. "I want you to have realistic expectations. It might not be somewhere either of us can stay. You can choose to stay here in the light without me if that's the case, or go back to your world, but living in my woods is not an option."

I charge him, pushing against his chest with all my might. He doesn't budge. "Don't I get a say? You captured me, dragged me here without my consent, and now you'll drag me back without it either?"

"I have to do what's best for you."

"I thought you said you loved me." My anger is gone. I tremble, my lip wobbles, and tears stream down my cheeks.

He softens, kneeling and cupping my chin in his giant clawed paw. "I do love you." I lock my eyes to his, still unsure if I'm imagining his words. "I love you more than myself. I can't bear to watch you suffer just to be with me."

I wrap my arms around his neck. "But I love you. I will suffer without you, more than I would in these woods."

He still doesn't melt into me, rigid as if not accepting my words. "You don't know that. You just met me, and I've nearly killed you numerous times, by my own hands, and simply putting you in the way of harm. You could forget all about me once you're home and safe."

I clench his fur. "I won't. I've never felt as safe as I do with you, even with monsters surrounding us. I've never had a home, never had a place I belong, but with you, I'm seen, complete, not damaged."

He doesn't respond, his eyes darting as if unsure how to react.

I jump him, wrapping my arms around his neck. "Please don't make me go. I can't live without you. I don't care what you think. I can't." I don't know when I became the type of girl that could be so desperate for a man, but maybe that's it. He's not a man. He's a monster, the dark and twisted kind that lights my nerves on fire, all while dulling the jagged edges of myself, healing my ragged wounds. I won't find anything like him back on Earth, and even if I could, I wouldn't want to. I want him. Only him, no matter what.

After what feels like a lifetime, he exhales, running a hand down my back. "Okay."

"Really?" I push against him to look at him, sadness completely gone.

He gives an incredulous look, shaking his head. "I won't make you do anything you don't want to do. I think I've done enough of that for a lifetime."

I hug him again and whisper into his ear. "I've always wanted everything you've done to me."

He growls, low in his throat, his grasp inching lower. I push back, already guessing where this is heading, and jump to the ground. I grab his hand. "Alright, Kitty, let's actually see what's beyond these woods." Probably should have done that before we had a big sap-fest, but I guess it's better this way. I want him to know that I'd choose him, even if my options were grim.

We stand at the edge again, hand in hand this time. "Do you want me to go first?" I ask.

"Of course not." He seems offended by the question and swoops me into his arms.

"But what if it burns?"

"I'm not putting you in harm's way, even if my fur turns to dust."

There's no sense arguing. I nod, staring straight ahead, holding onto him as he carefully makes his way down the steep hill. We're at the edge, the line of sunshine just a reach away. "I'll always love you," he says, and I look up to catch his searing gaze.

I pat his arm. "Good. And I love you. Now, let's go. I'm hoping there are cheeseburgers on the other side."

"What's a *cheeseburger*?"

"Way better than human screams, I can guarantee that."

"Nothing's better than your screams."

"Cheeseburgers first, and then you can make that call."

He chuckles, taking the first step forward. I hold my breath, hardly believing that this is the moment. I shut my eyes, a chicken shit thing to do since Scully should be more worried than I am, and he's the one carrying us out. Warmth coats my skin, and I gasp. I open my eyes to find sunshine all around me. We're still in woods, but there is grass and trees with green leaves.

"Scully!" I shout, sitting up and turning to him.

His eyes are clamped shut, and I laugh, studying him. "Are you burning?"

"No, but it's warm." He pops one eye open, the other quickly following. "What is this?"

"It's sunshine. Your mother was right. We're in a place with sunshine." I struggle out of his arms, an easy task since he's too in awe. My bare feet hit a paved road. "There must be a civilized species here. We should follow this path."

I step forward, but he yanks me back. "What if they're dangerous? Whoever lives here lives too close to the woods, too close to monsters."

"Monsters that can't get out because they'll burn from the sunlight. Maybe it's other monsters like you, monsters that found their humanity."

He sighs, shaking his head. "That's assuming a lot."

"I just really fucking want a cheeseburger and hope they have enough humanity to make me one."

"Fine. We came all this way. We might as well see what's at the end of this journey. But if they look at you like you're a cheeseburger, I'm slitting everyone's throat and carrying you out of here."

I pat his arm. "I don't doubt you will."

He grabs my hand and we walk, climbing over winding hills. It probably would be faster if he carried me, but I don't want to look defenseless to whoever we discover. I shouldn't be as excited as I am. Scully's right to have some reserve of what we might find. There's been nothing but terror in this realm. What makes me think there's anything rosier here? But so far, the blue sky, dotted with clouds, something like birds tweeting in the distance, can't make me think anything different. The more we walk and the longer the hope rolls around in my stomach, the more I start to worry. I'm already anticipating too much. I don't know if I can bear the heartbreak if this new place isn't anything but wonderful.

"Look," Scully says as we come over a hill. He's nearly two feet taller than me so he can see what's up ahead much quicker than I can. I scramble to catch up. In the distance sits a quaint town. Stone buildings surround cobbled roads, chimneys belch smoke, and laughter and voices bounce over the hilltops.

"I knew I smelled cheeseburgers." I can't take it anymore, I sprint ahead.

"Wait!" Scully calls, but there's no holding me back. The town looks even more human-like the closer I get. Perhaps this is the edge of the realm and we're back in some version of Earth. I slow, realization dawning over me. What would happen to Scully if humans lived here? Surely, they wouldn't welcome him with open arms?

By the time this very logical conclusion comes to mind, it's too late. I'm too close. A small building faces away, and the door opens with a ring from a bell above. I strain my eyes to catch what's leaving. A short, green circular figure walking on two legs, emerges, carrying a brown box in front of his large, singular eye. It's a monster, not like one I've seen in the forest, but they all seem to vary in appearance.

Scully catches up beside me, a low growl in his throat as we stare down the tiny green figure. The creature stops in his tracks, looking up and catching us in the distance. His eye appears to grow in size. Will he yell and run after us with razor-sharp teeth? I don't move, hoping Scully does the same so we can gauge his intentions.

The stillness breaks as the green beast raises a skinny arm and waves at us with a grin that takes up his whole face. "Hello!" he shouts. "Welcome to the light."

The words warm the last part of my heart, the part holding all my nerves. I breathe out, smiling, looking up to Scully.

He sighs, still staring at the stranger in the distance, growing closer, calling back to people coming out from their shops and homes.

"Well looks like you might get your cheeseburger after all," Scully says with a sigh.

I laugh, throwing my arms around him. He picks me up and I grab his face. "We're home."

"You're my home."

I kiss his mouth. It's the first time, and difficult around his fangs, but not any less amazing.

"Well, let's hope they don't try to eat us," Scully says, taking a step toward the village and townsfolk, seeming eager to greet us.

I shrug. "Hey, having people who want to eat you is not so bad."

"Only I get to eat you," he replies.

"I'll let them know."

"Good." He smiles.

I squint my eyes against the sun, my cheeks hurting from the happiness etched across my face and follow my monster to our new home.

Chapter 17: Scully

I still enjoy the darkness. I don't think that part of me will ever leave, and I'm grateful my new role allows me to indulge in my past affliction. There are parts of me that will never change, and as I sniff the forest air, catching her from beyond the border, my mind washes blank, just like before. I roar, racing through the foliage, pushing past the spindly trees and brush. I step past the darkness, and sunlight coats my fur, but it doesn't deter me; if anything, it urges me along as a symbol of her nearness.

The smell grows stronger with each step, blinding me to reason. Even in this state, I could stop myself, take calming breaths, but I have no desire. Only for her flesh on my lips, for her screams in my ear. It's been too long. I can't even remember the last time I heard the sweet melody. Perhaps last night? An unacceptable length of absence.

Noises from the town are barely a whisper as I race along the barrier, the darkness always close by. A billow of smoke snakes through the sky in front of me, a signal of my prey. A small cottage comes into view, but I don't bother bursting through the door. The smell wouldn't be so powerful if she were inside. I race toward the place she spends all her time on a clear day, the gated flower garden at the back of the small dwelling.

Her aroma nearly knocks me off my feet, and as I spot her, seated among the lilies, wiping a bead of sweat from her forehead, I can tell why. She's been soaking in her juices, pickling around her sweetness, all for me. Sitting in the sun and wafting her fumes for every beast nearby to enjoy. I should punish her for being such a temptation.

I roar, and her blue eyes pull away from the bulb halfway dug into the earth and lock on mine. She stands. "Scully, do not..." she doesn't finish, but picks up her white skirts and moves away from me as I barrel through the thin fence, sending shards of wood through the air.

"Come on! You just repaired that from last time!" she yells over her shoulder, increasing her speed and jumping over her rows of flowers. I may only have my animal instincts guiding me, but her love for her garden is enough to make me tread carefully so I don't harm her flowers. I'm cautious even if I don't slow.

She jumps over the low gate, her sunshine hair trailing behind her in a loose braid. With each movement, strands escape the intricate design, causing more of her to drift up my nostrils. I'm dizzy with hunger, but I push forward, increasing my speed, even if I'm still hindering myself to allow her the lead. It's no fun to chase her if I catch her right away.

She runs up a hill, grunting with the incline, but she doesn't slow down. Her elbows pump to propel her forward. "Scully, I'm making a pie!" she yells, the sound making its way to me behind her. "It's cooling on the windowsill." She stops, turns to me, now in the protection of an array of trees in the valley at the base of the hill. She waves her hands in front of her chest and takes small steps backwards. I slow as well, stalking her. Her face is flushed, and her chest heaves with violent breaths. "It's rhubarb. Your favorite."

I find my voice, the sound of it coming out so foreign to me. "Do you think I will change my mind for pie?"

She bundles her skirt again, probably realizing I can't be deterred. "And vanilla ice cream?"

I pretend to contemplate. "I would rather have you instead." I charge toward her. She screams and turns to run again, but I'm too fast, pulling her to the ground underneath me. I don't press all my weight down on her, pulling away slightly onto my knees. She takes the opportunity to crawl away from me, her ass hitting my crotch, already hard and wet, and my attachers searching the air for their haven.

I swoop an arm around her chest, pulling her back to me. "Trying to get away," I say through gritted teeth over the shell of her ear. "You know it only makes me want you more when you struggle." It's the truth. She loves this game, and she's playing her part perfectly. I may be a monster, but she wouldn't have me any other way. It's why I have no hesitation in slicing the threading between the leather material of her corset with one hand and with the other hiking her skirt over her ass and running my fingers through the sopping wet velvet between her legs. Her breasts pop free into my hand, moist and pebbled as I knead them. I can't wait to milk her one day, to drink the sweet liquid that will bead at her nipples when she's full of our children.

She moans quietly behind closed lips. Her heart pounds against my hand, and she still fights me, even as I position my tip at her wet entrance. My attachers grab her, and she can't suppress the sob this time. She cries out as she falls to the ground. My path is still clear, and I don't waste time thrusting inside of her, hard and fast, giving her no time to brace herself. She screams for me again, loud and glorious.

"Aren't you glad I wanted you more than a pie?" I ask, holding myself up on outstretched arms. Her face is smashed into the green grass, and she arches her back, her ass raised and welcoming me. I pull out again, my attachers stretch, and I pound into her, knocking her forward.

"It's good pie," she stutters around the words.

I tsk. "Still so fresh, even when I'm fucking the shit out of you." I go harder, pumping inside of her without caution, using her in the way she desires. She screams in a matter of seconds as I bottom out, filling her all the way through. The world washes around me. Power surges in my veins, and every bone melts into pure pleasure. I burst inside of her, coating every inch of her hot walls. My knot grows, and she moans again as I stretch her more.

I blanket her, careful not to let my weight drop. Now that I'm empty and my mind has cleared, I wish we were somewhere more comfortable. She's fertile, that's what I smelled through the woods. We talked about this the month before—we're ready for a child. I'm thankful for my knot to help keep my seed inside of her and hope that it lasts longer than usual to do so, but I also don't want my love pressed against the grass, ass up and uncomfortable.

"Are you okay?" I ask, brushing hair behind her ear.

She chuckles, her eyes closed. "Yes. Of course."

"What's funny?"

"Nothing. It's just funny that after fucking me like a ragdoll, you caress me and care for my comfort. Back to my Kitty, like always."

"Did you enjoy the chase?" I ask, growing self-conscious that she might be getting tired of our games.

She picks herself up, still attached, but turning her head to me with a serious expression. "Of course I do. And if I ever don't, I'll tell you. I promise." She pulls my hand to her lips with a kiss. I caress her cheek. "I love you."

"I love you too." I lean over her, capturing her lips with mine. It took a while to get the hang of kissing, but after we learned the techniques, it's one of my favorite activities, maybe even more than fucking sometimes. But only sometimes.

We're so lost in our embrace that I don't even notice when I pop free and spill onto the grass below us. I bundle her into my lap, not taking my lips off her.

"How was your patrol?" she asks, pulling away and caressing my jaw.

I shrug. "Good. I scared a few howlers away from the border, but I didn't find anyone on the brink of change."

"Maybe tomorrow," she offers.

Since coming to the town of Monsville, a lot has changed for us. The townspeople welcomed us with open arms. It turns out, I'm not the first monster to escape my haze and discover consciousness. Every member of the village was once a beast like me, lost in the darkness. There are also humans in the town, which delights my Marie. Everyone has a job, and mine is border patrol. Especially since we'll have little ones running close to the border, I make sure that any monsters with ill intent stay far away while also looking for anyone close to transforming into their true selves, and assisting them. It's a good gig, one that I wish existed when I was a child and my mother was so close to getting us out.

"Oh, I forgot to tell you. The girls are getting together for book club tonight, so they're all coming over."

I force a smile. "Sounds great." I'm glad that my Marie has friends. I know it's one of the reasons she's so happy here, but I can't help but wish their get-togethers were outside of our tiny home. I still enjoy my solitude, just now, my solitude with my Marie.

She hits my chest. "I can see right through you. Don't worry, it will only be Jill and Hannah tonight. Lucy and Traven aren't feeling well, first-trimester and all."

I cradle her jaw. "You can have whoever you want in our home. As long as you're happy, I am happy." I kiss her again, and she leans into me, her hands roaming over my patchy chest.

My cock stirs to attention. Perhaps trying for a baby again wouldn't be a horrible idea. I am hoping for a litter.

"Hello!" A voice calls from a distance. I tense, pulling Marie closer to me. Through the trees, I can see our house, the open kitchen window facing us. Wazco's bulbous eye pokes through the opening, and he waves a skinny hand in our direction. "Hope you don't mind, I let myself in. The door was open. Is it okay if I have a slice of this pie?" He uses a knife to cut a slice, not waiting for our answer.

"Fucking hell," I mutter, covering Marie with my body as she scrambles to fix her skirt and pull her broken corset back over her breasts. She laughs. "He may be a little forward, but he's sweet, and it's good you have a friend. Maybe you two can work on building the shed during my book club tonight." When she realizes the corset won't secure, she pulls it back off and puts it on backwards, sighing and standing.

I stand next to her, looking down at her golden hair so far away from me. "That guy is fucking clumsier than the chickens."

She laughs, slapping my chest. "Be nice. He was the first person to greet us to Monsville, and he made sure that we got the secluded house at the edge of town."

"Yeah, yeah." I take her small hand in mine, and we make our way back to our home.

She turns to me, walking backward. "I have an idea. We could make out a bunch in front of him to make him uncomfortable and leave." She winks.

My body heats. "What if he just wants to sit and watch? I know I would."

She laughs. "I guess there's only one way to find out." She pulls away from me, running ahead, looking back to make sure I'm following.

I don't chase her; instead, I capture the moment in memory. My beautiful Marie, running across the meadow. Sunlight dances across her skin, rosy with happiness. There's too much inside of me, a joy I never thought I'd experience.

She screams for me, tripping but catching herself before falling to the ground. Her laughter bubbles over the hills. There's always laughter now—always light shining through the darkness.

Thanks for Reading!

Thank you for reading! If you enjoyed *Scream for Me*, please make sure to leave a review. **Want some NSFW art of Scully's special member? Join G.M.'s Patreon!**

Want more of G.M. Fairy? Check out her other books...

Step Brother Bear: A Bear Shifter Lover Story

Her step-brother is an animal, and she is his prey.
Isabella has always hated her unruly step-brother, Derek.
Luckily for her, he spent most of their lonely upbringings
at a boarding school for troubled kids. Now that she's an
adult and back in her childhood home, she hates the tat-
tooed, moody man even more. Mostly because he's right
next door, set on making her life miserable and behav-
ing like a literal animal. Things get even worse when her
mom and step-dad leave town and task her to care for
the beast and his newly acquired gunshot wounds. Their
close quarters reveal heated secrets with monstrous conse-
quences. There's more to Derek than meets the eye, leaving Isabella to excavate terrifying and confusing feelings.
**Can she see past the claws, or will she decide the two
are just entirely different species?**

Pounded by Produce: A Veggie Love Tale

A tale of veggies tempted to break their vows. Fleeing a tumultuous past, Emily finds refuge at a kitchen job in a quiet countryside parish. Robert and Laurent are two best friends with a bond that has crossed lines throughout their history but now walk the straight and narrow, giving their lives to their parish as priests. One magical night under the harvest moon, Robert and Laurent experience a bizarre transformation: They wake up as a tomato and cucumber. Emily brings these ripe and juicy vegetables into the kitchen, but instead of preparing a meal, she uses them for other, more carnal needs. Emily awakens something inside of the priests, who switch back and forth between their human and vegetable forms. The three find themself in a steamy entanglement, unable to deny their primal desires. **Will they fight their urges or break their vows and alter the course of their lives forever?**

Stay up to date on all things G.M. Fairy!